# d r e a m e r s

# d r e a m e r s

## K n u t  H a m s u n

*Translated from the Norwegian by Tom Geddes*

A NEW DIRECTIONS CLASSIC

Copyright © 1996 by New Directions Publishing Corp.
Copyright 1904 by Gyldendal Norsk Forlag
English translation copyright © 1995 by Souvenir Press and Tom Geddes

First published in Norwegian under the title *Svaermere* by Gyldendal Norsk
Forlag, Oslo

Manufactured in the United States of America
New Directions Books are printed on acid-free paper
Published simultaneously in Canada by Penguin Books Canada Limited

Library of Congress Cataloging-in-Publication Data

Hamsun, Knut, 1859-1952
    [Sværmere. English]
    Dreamers / Knut Hamsun ; translated from the Norwegian by Tom
Geddes.
        p.    cm. — (New Directions classics)
    ISBN 0-8112-1321-8
    I. Geddes, Tom. II. Title    III.    Series
PT8950. H3S913    1996
839.8 ' 236—dc20                                95-52049
                                                     CIP

Celebrating 60 years publishing
for James Laughlin
by New Directions Publishing Corporation,
80 8th Avenue, New York 10011

dreamers

# 1

The housekeeper at the Vicarage, Marie van Loos, stood at the kitchen window looking out along the road. She knew the two people up by the gate very well: it was none other than her own fiancé, Rolandsen the telegraph-operator, and Olga the sexton's daughter. It was the second time she had seen the two of them together this spring — what could it mean? If she, Miss van Loos, had not had so many things to do just at that moment, she would have gone straight up the road to them and demanded an explanation.

But what time was there? The entire Vicarage was a hive of activity: the new parson and his wife were expected at any minute. Young Ferdinand had been stationed at an attic window to keep a look-out over the sea and warn of their arrival so that the coffee would be ready and hot. The travellers would need it after coming by boat all the way from the nearest steamer quay at Rosengaard, six miles away.

Some snow and ice still lingered on the meadows in the province of Nordland, but it was May now and fine weather, with long, bright days over these northerly regions of Norway. The crows and magpies were well advanced with their nests, and the bare hummocks were acquiring their first covering of new grass. In the garden the sallow was coming into bud even though still surrounded by snow.

The main question now was what kind of man the new parson would be. The whole village was on tenterhooks. Admittedly he was only coming as curate until a permanent incumbent was appointed; but in this poor fishing community, with the difficult journey to an outlying chapel every fourth Sunday, curates might find themselves staying for many years. It was certainly not a living in which anyone would be over-anxious to establish himself in the long term.

There was a rumour that the curate and his wife were wealthy people who did not have to watch every penny. They had already engaged a housekeeper and two maids in advance, and had not skimped on labour for the farm either, but had taken on two farmhands; and then there was young Ferdinand, who was supposed to be bright and intelligent and willing to run errands for them all. The congregation felt it to be a blessing that their parson was so well-to-do. And he was unlikely to be so precise every time in the matter of church-offerings and dues, but in fact might even give a little something to the poor himself. There was a great sense of excitement. The two lay-helpers and the other fishermen had all put in an appearance and were tramping up and down on the quay in their big boots, chewing tobacco and spitting, and gossiping among themselves.

Now at last Big Rolandsen came strolling down the road. He had left Olga, and Miss van Loos had turned away from her kitchen window. She would have it out with him later; it was not infrequently that she had to have words with Ove Rolandsen. She was of Dutch extraction, spoke with a Bergen accent and was so loquacious that her own fiancé had felt the need to give her the nickname of Miss Tongue-Loose. Rolandsen was always a jocular and impudent man.

Where was he going now? Did he really intend to be there to welcome the parson and his wife? He was probably no more sober now than he ever was, and there he came, with a sallow-bud in his button-hole and his hat a little askew, and that was how he planned to meet them! It was obvious that the lay-helpers down at the quay would rather he had not come at that particular moment, at such a very important moment.

Was it really right to look the way he did? His prominent nose was altogether too immodest for his humble position in life; and he let his hair grow right through the winter so that he appeared more and more artistic. His fiancée reacted by saying that he looked like a painter who had ended up as a photographer. He was now thirty-four, still a student and a bachelor; he

7

played the guitar and sang the local songs in his deep voice, laughing at all the sentimental parts till the tears ran. He wanted to create a grand impression. He was the manager of the telegraph-station, and had been in the same place for ten years. He was tall and powerfully built, and was not averse to a fight when the opportunity presented itself.

Suddenly young Ferdinand gave a start. From his attic window he had spotted the prow of Trader Mack's white launch speeding round the point; a second later he was down the stairs in three audacious leaps and yelling into the kitchen: 'Here they come!'

'Heavens, they're here already!' cried the maids in consternation. But the housekeeper remained calm and collected; she had worked for the previous vicar's family and had everything under control, efficient and competent as she was. 'Coffee on!' was all she said.

Young Ferdinand ran on out to the farmhands with the news. They dropped whatever they were holding, hurriedly pulled on their Sunday jackets and rushed down to the quay to see if they could help. There were now ten men in all to welcome the newcomers.

'Good morning,' called the parson from the stern, smiling slightly and doffing his soft hat. All the men on shore bared their heads respectfully, and the lay-helpers bowed so low that their long hair fell in their eyes. Big Rolandsen was less obsequious — he stood up straight, but doffed his hat very low.

The curate was a youngish man with ginger side-whiskers and freckles; his nostrils seemed to be stuffed with a profusion of fair hairs. His wife was lying prostrate in the deckhouse, seasick and exhausted.

'We've arrived,' said the curate through the doorway, going to help his wife out. They were both strangely dressed in thick old clothes that hardly looked presentable. But those must surely be just some odd outergarments they had borrowed for the journey, and their real clothes must be underneath. The lady's hat was pushed to the back of her head and her large eyes stared straight out at the men from her ashen face. Levion the lay-helper waded out and carried her ashore; the parson had to fend for himself.

'My name is Rolandsen, manager of the telegraph station,' said Big Rolandsen, stepping forward. He was fairly inebriated, and his eyes were glazed, but being a man of the world he was full of self-confidence. He was a hell of a character, no one had ever seen him at a loss when he had to mix with the gentry and bring out the grandiloquent phrases that were required. 'If I knew them all,' he said, turning to the curate again, 'I would introduce everyone to you. I think these two must be your lay-helpers. These two are your farm-hands. This is Ferdinand.'

The curate and his wife nodded to them all, 'Good morning, good morning.' They would soon come to know one another. The first task was to get their belongings ashore.

But Levion the lay-helper glanced back at the deckhouse, fully prepared to wade out again. 'Aren't there any little ones?' he asked.

Nobody responded: they all looked at the curate and his wife.

'No,' replied the skipper from the boat.

The lady blushed slightly.

The curate said: 'There are only the two of us . . . Come along and I'll settle up with you,'

A rich man, of course. A man who would not begrudge the poor their reward. The old vicar never settled up, he just said thanks — 'for the moment.'

They walked away from the sea, Rolandsen in the lead. He kept to the edge of the road, in the snow, to leave room for the others. He was wearing light, fashionable shoes, but seemed unperturbed; he even had his coat unbuttoned in the chilly May wind.

'So that's the church!' said the curate.

'It looks old. I don't suppose there's a stove in it?' asked his wife.

'I couldn't say,' Rolandsen replied, 'but I don't think so.'

The curate was taken aback. So it was not a churchgoer he had before him, but rather someone who made little distinction between weekdays and the Sabbath. He grew increasingly reserved towards this unknown man.

The housekeeper was standing on the steps and Rolandsen made the introductions once more. That done, he took his leave and turned to go. 'Wait a minute, Ove,' whispered Miss van Loos. Rolandsen did not wait, but again took his leave, and walked backwards down the steps. The curate thought him a very peculiar fellow.

His wife was already inside. She had recovered from her seasickness and was starting to look round the house. She allocated the brightest and most pleasant room to the curate for his study, and went on to claim for herself the bedroom that had formerly been occupied by Miss van Loos.

# 2

No, Rolandsen did not wait; he knew Miss van Loos and was aware of what would be in store for him. And he was always reluctant to do anything that went against his own inclinations.

Along the road he met one of the fishermen of the parish who had arrived too late to join in the welcome for the parson and his wife. It was Enoch, a meek and pious man who always walked with downcast eyes and a scarf around his head because of earache.

'You're too late,' said Rolandsen as he passed.

'Has he arrived?'

'Yes, he has. I've shaken hands with him.' Rolandsen called back over his shoulder: 'Mark my words, Enoch, I envy him his wife!'

He was just the man to address such careless and frivolous words to. Enoch was sure to spread them further.

Rolandsen walked on, skirting the forest until he came to the river. This was where Trader Mack's fish-glue factory was, and whenever Rolandsen passed by he liked to flirt with the girls who worked there. He was quite a Casanova, no doubt about it. He was in a very good mood today and stopped longer than usual. The girls could see that he was gloriously drunk.

'Well, Ragna, why do you think I come here so often?' asked Rolandsen.

'I've no idea,' Ragna answered.

'You must think I'm sent by old Laban.'

The girls giggled. 'When he says Laban he really means Adam.'

'I've come to save you,' said Rolandsen. 'You have to beware of the fishermen around here, they're out-and-out seducers!'

'There's no greater seducer than you,' said another girl. 'You've got two kids already. You ought to be ashamed of yourself.'

'How can you talk like that, Nicoline? You've always been a thorn in my flesh and you'll be the death of me, you know damned well. But as for you, Ragna, I'm going to save your soul whether you like it or not!'

'You go off to your Miss van Loos,' retorted Ragna.

'You're so totally lacking in sense,' Rolandsen went on. 'For instance, how many hours do you steam those fish-heads before you screw down the valve?'

'Two hours,' Ragna replied.

Rolandsen nodded. He had estimated about that and had already worked it out. Yes, that devil

Rolandsen was fully aware of why he took that walk up to the factory every day to sniff about and chat up the girls.

'Don't take that lid off, Pernilla,' he suddenly shouted. 'Are you mad?'

Pernilla flushed. 'Fredrik said I was to stir it,' she replied.

'Every time you lift the lid, you lose the heat in the steam,' said Rolandsen.

But when Fredrik Mack, the trader's son, arrived on the scene a few moments later, Rolandsen resumed his usual bantering tone:

'Wasn't it you, Pernilla, who was in service with the mayor for a year? You were so grumpy and bad-tempered all the time that the only thing you didn't smash to pieces was the bedclothes!'

They all laughed. Pernilla was actually the gentlest creature on earth. She also suffered from poor health, and as daughter of the organ-blower in the church she had a slight aura of saintliness about her.

Emerging on to the road once more, Rolandsen caught sight of Olga the sexton's daughter again. She must have been to the shop. She was hurrying away in order to avoid him — it would be shameful if Rolandsen should think she had been waiting for him. But Rolandsen had no such thoughts at all, he knew that if he did not actually manage to come face to face with this young girl she would always slip away from him and disappear. Not that he minded failing to get any-where with her, not in the least; she was not the one who occupied his mind.

He came home to the telegraph station, and affected his most supercilious manner in order not to be bothered by his assistant telegraphist, who would be looking forward to a chat. Rolandsen was not a convivial colleague these days. He locked himself in his little side room that no one but he and an old woman ever entered. That was where he lived and slept.

That room was Rolandsen's world. Rolandsen was not just irresponsibility and inebriation, he was also a great thinker and inventor. There was a smell of acids and chemicals and medicines in his room, an odour that permeated the corridor and came to the notice of every visitor. Rolandsen made no secret of the fact that he had all these medicaments there solely to disguise the aroma of all the brandy he consumed. But this was part of an act designed purely to give himself an air of inscrutability.

The truth was that he used all these liquids in bottles and jars for his experiments. He had discovered a new chemical process for the manufacture of fish-glue; his new method would wipe Trader Mack's off the face of the earth. Mack had set up his factory at considerable expense, his means of transport were inadequate and his raw materials restricted to the fishing season. And the business was managed by his son Fredrik, who was no expert. Rolandsen could produce fish-glue from many substances in addition to fish-heads, even from the waste materials that Mack discarded. And from the final residue he could also extract a remarkable dye.

If only Rolandsen the telegraph-operator had not had to struggle with his overwhelming poverty and inadequacy, his invention would by now have become reality. But nobody could get hold of money in this place except through Trader Mack, and for obvious reasons he could not approach him. He had once ventured to suggest that the glue was too expensive to produce from the factory up at the waterfall; but Mack had simply dismissed the idea with a wave of his hand in his grand and extravagant manner and remarked that the factory was a gold-mine. Rolandsen was burning to demonstrate the results of his calculations. He had sent samples of his product to chemists both at home and abroad, and had been assured that it was a good start. But he got no further. He still had to present the pure, clear liquid to the world, and take out patents in all countries.

So it was not for nothing that Rolandsen had gone down to the quayside today to take part in the reception of the curate and his wife. Sly old Rolandsen had his motives. If it were true that the curate was wealthy, he might well invest a little money in a significant and infallible invention. 'If no one else will, then I will!' was what he was sure to say—at least that was what Rolandsen hoped.

Alas, Rolandsen was ever hopeful; it took very little to rouse his expectations. But it had to be admitted that he was also good at bearing disappointments; he was proud and resilient and his spirit was never broken.

Even Mack's daughter Elise had not broken his spirit. She was a tall, attractive girl, with a dark complexion and rosy lips, twenty-three years old. It was rumoured that Captain Henriksen of the coastal steamer secretly adored her; but the years went by and nothing came of it. What could the problem be? Rolandsen had already made a complete fool of himself for her sake three years before when she was only twenty and he had thrown himself at her feet. She had been tactful enough to profess not to understand him. That was the point at which Rolandsen should have stopped and withdrawn; but he persisted, and last year had begun to speak openly. She was forced to laugh in his face to make this presumptuous telegraph-operator realise the gulf that lay between them. Was she not the lady who had kept even Captain Henriksen waiting for years for her consent? So Rolandsen had gone straight off and got engaged to Miss van Loos. He was not a man to be mortified by rejection, even from the highest quarters.

But now it was spring again. And spring was almost unbearable for sensitive hearts. It drove creation to its utmost limits, it wafted its spice-laden breath even into the nostrils of the innocent.

# 3

The spring herring were moving in from the open sea. All day long the skippers were scanning the waters through binoculars from their boats. The herring were to be found where the birds flocked and kept swooping down to dive into the waves. The fish were already being caught in drift nets out in deep water, but now the question was whether they would make their way into the shallows, into the bays and fjords where they could be trapped and caught in seine nets. Then the excitement and commotion and shouting would begin, with a huge turn-out of people and boats of all kinds. And the profits earned would be as plentiful as the sands of the ocean.

The fisherman is a gambler. He lays his drift nets or lines and waits for the catch, he casts his seine nets and lets fate take its course. He often suffers loss upon loss, his gear may sink or be swept away in storms; but he re-equips himself and sets out again. Sometimes he sails further afield, to where he has heard that fortune has smiled on others, struggling to row for weeks across treacherous seas, only to arrive too late: the game is over. But now and again the big prize may be lying in wait for him to stop him in his tracks and fill his boat with riches. No one knows whom luck will favour, everyone has the same grounds for hope . . .

Trader Mack was ready, his nets were in the boat and his skipper never took his binoculars from his eyes. Mack had a ketch and two sloops lying at anchor in the bay, just emptied and cleaned after their voyage to Lofoten with dried cod. He would load them with herring if the herring came; his store-loft was full of empty barrels. He would also buy up all the herring he could lay hands on, and had already provided himself with enough cash so that he could step in before the prices rose.

In the middle of May Mack's net made its first catch. Not much, just fifty barrels; but the news spread, and a day or two later there was a crew in the bay from elsewhere. The chances here seemed good.

Then one night there was a burglary at Mack's office in the factory. It was a very daring crime: the nights were now as bright as day from evening till morning and everything that happened could be seen from afar. The thief had broken open two doors and stolen two hundred crowns.

It was a completely unprecedented event in the village, beyond all comprehension. Even the elderly had never in their lives known of a burglary at Mack's place. The people of the village might steal and cheat in a petty way, but they would never have attempted a theft on that scale. Immediately, it was the non-local fishing crew who were suspected and questioned.

But they were able to prove that they had been five miles away from the factory on the night of the burglary, with a full crew, searching for herring along the open coast.

Mack was extremely upset. This meant that one of the villagers must have committed the crime.

He was not so concerned about the money, and stated quite frankly that the thief was stupid not to have taken more. But to think that any of his neighbours could steal from *him*, that really hurt him as their omnipotent lord and protector. Was it not he who provided half the local community budget with the tax on his various enterprises? And had any deserving case ever left his office empty-handed?

Mack offered a reward for information that might help solve the crime. There were new boats coming in now almost daily, and these outsiders would form an odd impression of Mack's relationship with his people if it was thought they were stealing his money. Like the generous and lordly merchant that he was, he fixed the reward at four hundred crowns. He wanted everyone to see that it did not have to be an exactly equivalent amount.

The new parson heard tell of the burglary, and on

Trinity Sunday, when the sermon was to be about Nicodemus who came to Jesus by night, he took the opportunity to deliver an attack on the thief. 'They come to us by night,' he said, 'and break down our doors and steal our property. Nicodemus did no wrong, he was a timid man and chose the night to go about; but his business concerned his soul. What do people do now? The world has descended into shamelessness, the night is used for plunder and sin. Let the guilty person be struck down! Bring him forth!'

The parson was proving to be a fighting cock. This was the third time he had preached and he had already inspired many of the sinners in the parish to repent. When he stood in the pulpit he looked so pallid and transformed that he resembled a lunatic. There were some in the congregation who had had enough even on the first Sunday and did not dare come again. Even Miss van Loos was shaken, though her own tongue was as sharp as a knife and she had used it to good effect for years. The two maids under her were pleased to notice the change.

Quite a few people had arrived in the area now. It has to be admitted that some of them were delighted at Trader Mack's humiliation. Mack had become much too powerful, with both his big trading posts, his nets, his factory and his numerous boats. The other fishermen would rather stick by their own traders, who were affable and egalitarian and wore neither white collars nor deerskin gloves as Mack did. The burglary was a fitting repayment for all his pretentiousness. Nor did

21

they approve of his offering such great sums for this, that and the other; he might need his cash for buying up herring if the herring came. He was hardly a rich enough man to have infinite amounts of money like the stars in the sky. Good Lord, perhaps the theft had been carried out by Mack himself or his son Fredrik, to make it look as if he could afford to scatter money like grass seed when he was actually in financial difficulties! That was the substance of the gossip on the boats and on shore.

Mack realised that he would have to demonstrate that he was still a man of means. There were people from five parishes here now who would recount their impressions to their trading contacts and families back home. Rumours would spread far and wide about the sort of man Mack of Rosengaard was.

The next time he had to visit the factory, Mack hired a steamer for the journey. It was five or six miles from the regular landing stage and it cost him good money, but he did not let that deter him. There was a great bustle on shore when the ship steamed in carrying Mack and his daughter Elise. He was the ship's master, so to speak, and stood on board in his fur coat and with his huge red scarf wrapped round him, even though it was a warm summer's day. As soon as father and daughter had been put ashore, the ship turned and made off: everyone could see that it had come entirely on account of him. Even many of the outsiders there had to admit Mack's supremacy.

But Mack did more than that. He could not forget the disgrace of the burglary. He put up a new poster, promising the thief himself the four hundred crowns if he gave himself up. Such magnanimity was without compare. Everyone could surely see now that it was not the wretched stolen money itself that Mack was trying to recover. But it did not stop the gossip passing from mouth to mouth: 'If the thief is who I think he is, this isn't likely to make him turn himself in, either. But don't say that I said so!'

The eminent Mack was in an impossible position. His reputation was being eroded. He had been eminent for twenty years, and everyone had deferred to him with respect; but now it seemed as if people were not greeting him with as much deference as before. Despite the fact that he had been decorated with a Royal Order. What hadn't he achieved! He was the spokesman for the village, the fishermen idolised him, the small traders on the open coast tried to imitate him. Mack had stomach trouble, probably caused by his regal lifestyle, and he used to wear his broad red scarf around his waist as soon as it was even slightly chilly. The traders up the coast also wrapped red scarves around themselves, those little upstarts who only survived by Mack's good grace. They wanted to be taken for great men too, who ate such sumptuous repasts that they got stomach ache. Mack went to church in shoes that creaked and walked ostentatiously up the aisle; even his creaky shoes were emulated by others.

Some actually soaked their shoes in water and dried them out ready for Sunday so that they would creak well on the church floor. Mack was the supreme paradigm for everything.

# 4

Rolandsen was sitting in his room, busy with his experiments. From the window he noticed that a particular branch of a particular tree in the forest was swaying up and down. There must be someone shaking it, but the foliage had grown too dense for him to see anything. So he carried on working.

But his work was not going at all well today. He tried plucking at his guitar and singing one of his witty laments, but he got no pleasure from that, either. Spring was here, and Rolandsen was restless.

Elise Mack had arrived; he had met her the previous evening. He was proud and haughty and had decided how he would behave towards her. She seemed to want to be friendly, and made a few cheerful remarks, but he was not receptive.

'I bring you greetings from the telegraph-operators

at Rosengaard,' she said.

Rolandsen would not have described the telegraph-operators as friends, it was not as if he was a colleague of theirs. She was only trying to stress the distance between herself and him again—but he would get his own back and make her pay for it.

'You must teach me to play the guitar a little one day,' she said.

Now that was a slight surprise, and he should have been rather gratified; but he would not accept her overtures. He would respond in kind.

'Certainly. Whenever you like. You can have my guitar.'

That was the way to treat her. As if she were not Elise Mack, a lady who could afford ten thousand guitars.

'No thanks,' she said. 'But we could practise on it.'

'You can have it.'

She tossed her head and replied:

'I'm sorry, I don't want it.'

His attitude had offended her. He began to draw back from his desire for revenge and mumbled:

'I just wanted to give you the only thing I possess.'

He doffed his cap with a grand flourish and continued on his way.

He went to the sexton's house to look for Olga. Now that it was spring Rolandsen had to have a sweetheart; it was no easy matter to hold his own great heart in check. But he also had a special reason for paying court to Olga. There was talk of Fredrik Mack having become interested in the sexton's daughter, and Rolandsen desired nothing so much as to put him right out of the picture. Fredrik was Elise's brother, and a rejection would do the family no harm. But also Olga was rather desirable anyway. Rolandsen had seen her growing up from a small child. There was not much money to spare in her house and she had always had to wear her clothes right out before getting any new ones, but she was lively and pretty and her shyness was very endearing.

Rolandsen had met her on two successive days. The only way he could continue to meet her so often was by actually going to her home on the pretext of lending her father a book every day. He had to force these books on the sexton, who neither wanted nor understood them. Rolandsen had to stand there and expatiate enthusiastically on their merits. 'They're the most useful books in the world,' he would say, 'I want to let people know about them and spread them around.'

He asked the sexton if he could cut hair. But the sexton had never done anything like that in his life; it was Olga who cut everyone's hair in the house. So Rolandsen made fervent pleas to Olga to cut his. She blushed and ran away and hid. 'I can't,' she said. But Rolandsen discovered her hiding-place, and bombarded her with so many eloquent and persuasive arguments that she finally gave in.

'How do you want it?' she asked.

'Just as *you* like,' he replied. 'How else would I have it?'

Then he turned his attention to the sexton and so bothered and wearied the old man with intricate questions that he had to seek sanctuary in the kitchen.

Rolandsen started showing off and became increasingly grandiloquent:

'When you emerge from the darkness of a winter evening and enter a lighted room, radiance floods into your face from all around.'

Olga had no idea what he meant, but said 'Yes.'

'Yes,' said Rolandsen. 'And the same thing happens to me when I come to see you.'

'I'd better not cut any more off here, had I?' asked Olga.

'Yes, go on cutting. Do it the way you want. You thought you could just go and hide, didn't you, but it didn't make things any better for me. It's like lightning trying to put out a spark.'

He was beginning to sound slightly crazy.

'If you could only keep your head still, I'd be able to do it better,' she said.

'Then I wouldn't be able to look at you. Tell me, have you got a boy-friend?'

Olga was totally taken aback. She was not yet old or experienced enough not to be embarrassed by some things.

'Me? No,' was all she could say. 'I think it'll have to do like this. I'll just even it up a little.' She felt she had to speak nicely to him because she suspected he was drunk.

But Rolandsen was not drunk, he was totally sober.

He had been very busy the last few days: the numbers of fishing boats from elsewhere had brought a lot of work to the telegraph station.

'No, don't stop,' he begged. 'Just trim it round again a couple of times — please do!'

Olga laughed. 'No, there's hardly anything left as it is.'

'Oh, your eyes are like twin stars,' he said, 'and when you smile at me I'm bathed in sunlight.'

She removed the cloth and brushed him down, then gathered up the hair from the floor. He jumped down to help her, and their hands touched. She was so young; he could feel her breath, and a warm thrill went through him. He seized her hand. He noticed that her dress was fastened at the neck with just an ordinary safety pin. It looked quite poverty-stricken.

'No — why are you doing that?' she stammered.

'No reason. Well, simply to thank you for cutting my hair. If I weren't firmly and eternally committed to someone else, I would be falling in love with you.'

She stood up with the hair clippings in her hands, and he moved back.

'Now your clothes will be in a mess,' she said as she went out of the door.

When the sexton came in Rolandsen had to look cheerful again; he stretched his cropped head forward and pulled his hat down over his ears to show how big it was for him now. Then he suddenly glanced at the clock, said he had to be back at the telegraph office, and hurried away.

He went straight to the store. He asked to see some clasps and brooches, the best and most expensive there were. He chose an imitation cameo and requested credit—but he was refused: he owed too much already. So he had to take a cheap agate-coloured glass brooch that he could pay for out of his small change. And off he went with his treasure.

That had been the previous evening . . .

Now Rolandsen sat in his room, unable to concentrate on his work. He put on his hat and went out to see who was in the forest shaking the branches. He walked straight into the lion's jaws: it was Miss van Loos signalling to him and now standing waiting for him. He should have restrained his curiosity.

'Good morning,' she said. 'What a sight your hair looks.'

'I always have it cut in the spring,' he replied.

'I cut it for you last year. This year I wasn't good enough, I suppose.'

'I don't want to quarrel with you,' he said.

'You don't?'

'No. And you shouldn't be standing here tearing up the whole forest by its roots where everyone can see you.'

'And you shouldn't stand there trying to be funny,' she retorted.

'You ought to be down the road waving on olive branch at me,' Rolandsen went on.

'Did you cut your hair yourself?'

'Olga cut it.'

The girl who might one day be the wife of Fredrik Mack, that's who had cut his hair — and he had no wish to conceal the fact, but would rather trumpet it abroad.

'Olga, did you say?'

'Why not? Her father couldn't do it.'

'You're pushing me too far: our relationship is going to come to an end one fine day,' said Miss van Loos.

He stood thinking about that for a moment.

'It might be for the best,' he said at last.

'What are you saying!' she cried.

'What am I saying? That you're completely out of your mind in the spring, that's what I'm saying. Look at me, do I show any signs of spring fever?'

'But you're a man,' was her only answer. 'Anyway, I won't put up with all this nonsense about Olga.'

'Is it true that the new vicar is rich?' he asked.

Miss van Loos wiped her eyes and was her usual confident and practical self again.

'Rich? I think he's as poor as a church mouse.'

Rolandsen's hopes were dashed.

'You should see his clothes,' she continued. 'And his wife's. Some of her skirts . . . But he's a superb vicar. Have you heard him preach?'

'No.'

'He's one of the most best preachers I've ever heard,' said Miss van Loos in her Bergen dialect.

'Are you sure he's not rich?'

'Well, he's been up at the store asking for credit.'

Rolandsen's world darkened momentarily and he

turned to leave.

'Are you going?' she asked.

'Yes. What did you actually want me for?'

What a nerve! She had already been influenced by the new curate to some extent, and had been endeavouring to develop meekness; but now her former nature reasserted itself.

'I'll tell you something,' she said, 'you're really going too far.'

'All right.'

'You're doing me a cruel wrong.'

'Maybe,' said Rolandsen in the same vein.

'I can't bear it any longer; I'm going to finish with you.'

Rolandsen gave the matter some further consideration. Then he said:

'I thought it would come to this one day. On the other hand, I'm not God: there's nothing I can do about it. You do what you like.'

'If that's the way you want it,' she said angrily.

'You weren't so indifferent that first evening up here in the forest. I kissed you, and the only sound you made was a dear little squeak.'

'I certainly didn't squeak,' she said with indignation.

'And I fell in love with you for ever, and thought you would be really special. So much for that!'

'Don't worry about me,' she said bitterly. 'But what will happen to you?'

'To me? No idea. I don't care any more.'

'You needn't expect anything to come of you and
Olga. She'll have Fredrik Mack.'

So, said Rolandsen himself, it was already common
knowledge. He began to move off, deep in thought,
and Miss van Loos went with him. They came down
on to the road and kept on walking.

'Short hair suits you,' she said. 'But it's been badly
cut, really uneven.'

'Could you lend me three hundred crowns?' he
asked.

'Three hundred crowns?'

'Just for six months.'

'I wouldn't lend you the money anyway. It's obviously all over between us now.'

He nodded. 'If that's the way you want it.'

But when they reached the gate of the Vicarage,
where Rolandsen would leave her, she said: 'I'm sorry,
I don't have that amount of money to give you.' She
proffered her hand. 'I daren't stand here long: goodbye
for the present.' She took a few steps and then turned
and asked: 'Isn't there anything else you'd like me to
say?'

'No, what might there be?' he replied. 'Nothing new
since last time.'

She went in. Rolandsen felt a sense of relief and
hoped this really was the end.

There was a notice on the gatepost and Rolandsen
read it; it was Trader Mack's announcement about the
burglary: Four hundred crowns for information. The

reward would even be paid to the thief himself if he came forward and gave himself up.

Four hundred crowns! thought Rolandsen to himself.

# 5

No, the new curate was not rich, far from it. It was just that his hapless young wife had brought with her the carefree ways of the wealthy from her family home and wanted lots of servants around her. And she had nothing to do; she had no children, and she had never learned how to do housework, so she spent her time thinking up childish schemes in her little head. She was a sweet and lovely cross that the the household had to bear.

Heavens above, how tirelessly the good parson had fought ludicrous battles with his wife to teach her some sense of order and consideration! He had worked on her in vain for four years. He picked up threads and papers from the floor, put ᵗhings in their rightful place, closed doors after her, saw to the stoves, and adjusted the ventilators. When his wife went out he would go on a tour of the rooms and see how she had left them: hairpins here, there and everywhere, combs full of hair, handkerchiefs all over the place, chairs piled high with clothes. He suppressed his feeling of anger and went round putting it all straight. He had felt less homeless as a bachelor in his attic room than he did now.

At first he had begged and scolded, to some effect; his wife would admit that he was right and promise to mend her ways. Then she would rise early the next morning and start tidying feverishly: the child in her would develop a spurt of seriousness, she would play at being grown-up and would do so to excess. But the energy would quickly evaporate, and a few days later the house would be in the same state as before. She never wondered how things kept getting into such a mess; on the contrary, she was always surprised when her husband again began to express his perpetual discontent. 'I knocked over that dish and smashed it, but it didn't cost much,' she would say. 'The pieces have been lying there since this morning,' he would point out.

One day his wife told him that Oline the maid would have to go. Oline had reproached her for removing articles from the kitchen and leaving them lying wherever she last happened to be using them.

Gradually the curate became hardened to it and stopped his daily complaining; instead he went round tight-lipped and with as few words as possible, tidying and clearing everything up. And his wife did not even notice it, she was used to having someone clear away after her. Her husband sometimes actually thought she was to be pitied. She was always so pleasant, despite being half-starved and badly dressed; she never even uttered a sigh about her poverty, although she had been used to having whatever she wanted. She would sit sewing and altering dresses that had been altered many times before, humming contentedly like a little girl. But then suddenly the child in her would come to the fore again and she would leave her needlework, drop everything in a muddle and go out for a walk. Chairs and tables might be covered in pieces of unpicked dress material for days. Where did she go? She still had the habit from her childhood home of flitting round the shops, she loved buying things. She could always find a use for remnants of material, scraps of ribbon, combs, perfumes, toothpowder, small metal objects, matchboxes and pipes to blow through. Why didn't she just buy one big thing, the curate thought, no matter how expensive it was, even if it got him into debt? He could try and write a short popular history of the Church and pay for it that way.

So the years went by. There were often quarrels, but the couple were still fond of each other, and as long as the curate did not interfere too much everything went reasonably well. But he had the annoying habit of keeping an eye on household affairs even from a distance, even from the window of his study. Only the day before, he had noticed that it was raining on a couple of bedspreads hanging out in the garden. He wondered whether he should call someone, but then he suddenly saw his wife returning; she had been out and was now coming home because of the rain. He had a feeling she would not take the bed covers in with her, and sure enough she went straight up to her room. The curate called to the kitchen, but there was nobody there, and he could hear Miss van Loos at work in the dairy. He went out himself and carried the covers in.

And there the matter might have rested. But the curate, an inveterate nagger, could not hold his tongue. In the evening his wife asked for the covers, and they were brought.

'They're wet!' she exclaimed.

'They'd have been even wetter if I hadn't brought them in,' said the curate.

At that she turned on him. 'Was it you who brought them in? There was absolutely no need for you to, I would have told the maids myself.'

He gave a bitter smile. 'Then the bedspreads would still be out there now.'

His wife was upset. 'Is there any point in making such a fuss over a few drops of rain? You're completely impossible all day long, you nag me about everything!'

'I wish I didn't have to keep on nagging you,' he replied. 'Just look at your wash-bowl there, lying on the bed.'

'I had to put it there because there wasn't room any-where else.'

'Even if you had another wash-stand, it would soon be piled high.'

His wife lost her temper. 'My God, how unreasonable you are! You must be ill. I can't bear it any longer!' She sat down and just stared straight in front of her.

But she did bear it. Moments later it was all forgotten; her generous heart forgave the injustice. She had such a happy and cheerful disposition.

The curate kept more and more to his study, where the disorder of the rest of the house did not impinge. He was tough and strong, a real work-horse. He had asked the lay-helpers about the moral life of the village, and what he heard did not please him at all. He wrote letters of admonition and exhortation to a number of his parishioners; and where these had no effect he went on personal visits to the transgressors. He was a man who commanded fear and respect. And he spared no one. He had found out for himself that one of his own helpers, Levion, had a sister who was easy-going and rather too accommodating to the fishermen: she also received a letter. He summoned her brother and entrusted him with the letter and a specific message: 'Give her that. And tell her that I shall keep a sharp eye on her activities in future.'

One day Trader Mack came to see the curate, who showed him into the parlour. It was a short, but significant, visit. He wanted to let the curate know that if assistance was ever needed for anyone in the village, he was more than willing to help. The curate was grateful and delighted. If he had not been sure of it before, he could now be certain that Mack of Rosengaard was indeed the protector of them all. The old gentleman was so authoritative and elegant that even the curate's wife, who had been brought up in a town, was impressed. He was a man of stature, and those stones in his shirt-pin were undoubtedly genuine.

'The fishing's going well,' said Mack. 'We've had another catch. Well, it's not all that significant really, just twenty barrels or so, but it mounts up with what's gone before. So I thought it was an appropriate time to remember our duty to our neighbours.'

'That's right,' cried the curate rapturously. 'That's how it should be! Is twenty barrels a small catch? I've got no idea of such matters.'

'Well, two or three thousand barrels would be better.'

'Two or three thousand!' exclaimed the curate's wife.

'But what I don't catch myself, I buy from others,' Mack continued. 'A boat from the outer islands made a good catch yesterday, and I bought it up straight away. I'm going to fill every boat I've got with herring.'

'You've evidently got a very extensive business,' said the curate.

Mack admitted that it was becoming so. It was actually an old-established inherited business, he said, but he had expanded it and branched out into new fields. Everything he did, he did for his children.

'Heavens above, how many workshops and factories and stores have you actually got, then?' the curate's wife asked in excitement.

Mack laughed. 'Well, I can't really say offhand, Ma'am. I'd have to count.'

He forgot his trials and tribulations for a while as they chatted; he was by no means averse to being asked about his business interests.

'If only we lived near your big bakery at Rosengaard,' said the curate's wife, with her own housekeeping problems in mind. 'The bread we bake is so awful.'

'There's a baker at the mayor's house.'

'Yes, but he never has any bread.'

The curate put in: 'Unfortunately he drinks too much. I've written him a letter, but . . .'

Mack sat in silence for a while. Then he said: 'I'll set up a bakery here, then, in the local branch of my store.'

He was omnipotent, he could do whatever he liked. One word from him and a bakery sprang up then and there.

'Just think!' exclaimed the curate's wife, her eyes round with wonder.

'You'll be all right for bread, Ma'am. I'll telegraph straight away to get some people over. It'll take a little while, a week or two.'

The curate remained silent. That would make the bread dearer. Couldn't the maids bake all the bread they needed?

'I must thank you for so generously granting me credit at your store,' he said.

'Yes,' his wife added, becoming thoughtful once again.

'Only too pleased,' said Mack. 'Anything you want—I'm at your service.'

'It must be quite a responsibility having as much power over everything as you have,' she said.

'I certainly don't have power over everything. For instance, I can't find the thief who burgled me.'

'That affair really was too bad!' exclaimed the curate. 'You promise a big reward, a fortune, and still the thief doesn't give himself up.'

Mack shook his head.

'It's also the basest ingratitude to steal from *you*,' added the curate's wife.

Mack agreed. 'Since you mention it, Ma'am, I certainly wouldn't have expected it. Indeed I wouldn't. I can't think that I've treated my people so badly.'

The curate remarked: 'The fact is that people steal wherever there's something to be stolen. The thief knew where to go.'

The curate, in his naive way, had said exactly the right thing. Mack felt better again. Viewed like that, all the indignity of the theft seemed much less.

'But everyone's going round gossiping,' he said. 'It's harming my interests and upsetting me. There are so many strangers here now, and they're no respecters of persons. And my daughter Elise has taken it to heart.

'Well,' he continued, getting up, 'it will all pass over. But as I said, if you come across any cases of hardship in the parish, please remember me.'

Mack took his leave. He had formed a very good impression of the curate and his wife, and would speak well of them to everyone. That would not do them any harm. Or would it? How far had the gossip about him spread? His son Fredrik had come home yesterday and said that a drunken fisherman had shouted to him from a boat: 'Have you given yourself up and claimed the reward yet?'

# 6

The days were getting warmer now, and the herring catches had to stay in the nets in order not to spoil; they could only be emptied out when it rained or on cool nights. There were few fish left now anyway, the year was too far advanced, and the boats were beginning to leave. Besides, the spring ploughing and sowing had to be done back home, which would require all the available men.

The nights too were bright and sunny. It was weather for dreamers, for young people to flit about in restless excitement. They wandered the roads at night, singing and beating the air with sallow-twigs. And from all the isles and skerries came the sound of birds: guillemots and oyster-catchers and gulls and eider-ducks. The seal thrust his dripping head up out of the water and looked around, then dived back down again to his own world.

Ove Rolandsen too was dreaming in his own way. Occasional singing and the notes of a guitar were audible from his room by night, which was more than might be expected from a man of his age. Nor was it purely for pleasure that he plucked the strings and sang, but rather to distract himself and provide some relief from his worrying problems. Rolandsen was thinking, with as much effort as he could muster; he was in a great quandary and had to find a way out. Miss van Loos had returned to him again, of course; she was not one to squander love and was intent on keeping their engagement going. On the other hand, he was not God, he could not contain his heart if it insisted on flying away in the spring. It was a burden to have a fiancée who did not understand a clean break.

Rolandsen had been to the sexton's house once more, and Olga was sitting outside the door. But herring were now a crown a barrel, times were good, and much money had come into the parish; it all seemed to have gone to Olga's head. Or was something else the matter with her? Was Rolandsen perhaps a man one could equally well do without? She merely glanced up at him and carried on with her knitting.

Rolandsen said: 'Ah! You looked up. Your eyes are like daggers, they pierce my soul.'

'I don't understand you,' said Olga.

'Well, do you think I understand myself any better? I'm going out of my mind. By standing here now I'm just making it easier for you to torment me more through the coming night.'

'Don't stand there, then.'

'I was listening to a voice inside me last night. Its words were unrepeatable. To cut a long story short, I resolved immediately to make an important decision, if you think it would be the right thing.'

'Me? How can it have anything to do with me?'

'Well, well,' said Rolandsen, 'you're very sour today, just sitting there and fending me off. You won't be able to keep your hair on soon, you're getting so big-headed.'

Olga was silent.

'Did you know that Børre the organ-blower has a daughter whom I could get if I wanted?'

Olga stared at him and burst out laughing.

'No, don't sit there smiling like that—it makes me even more infatuated with you.'

'You're completely mad!' said Olga in a low voice, blushing deeply.

'Sometimes I think to myself: perhaps she laughs at me just to increase my torment. That's how they kill ducks and geese, by stabbing them in the head first, so that they swell up and are twice as tasty.'

Olga sounded offended. 'Of course I don't, you needn't think anything of the sort.' And she rose and started to go indoors.

'If you go in I'll follow you and ask your father if he's read those books,' said Rolandsen.

'My father isn't at home.'

'Well—I didn't come to see him anyway. But you're surly and stand-offish today, Olga. It's impossible to get a friendly word out of you. Your'e just trying to ignore me and put me down.'

Olga laughed again.

'Børre has a daughter, as I said,' Rolandsen went on. 'Her name's Pernilla. I've been there and made enquiries. Her father pumps the organ in church.'

'Do you want a girl-friend on every finger?' asked Olga with candour.

'My fiancée was Marie van Loos,' he replied, 'but we've broken things off. You can ask her yourself. She'll probably be going away soon.'

'Yes, mother, I'm coming,' Olga called, through the window.

'Your mother didn't call you, she only looked at you.'

'Yes, but I know what she meant.'

'All right then. I'll go. But Olga, you know what *I* mean as well, but you don't give me the same answer, to say that you're coming.'

She opened the door to go in. She must have got the impression by now that he was not the masterful Rolandsen he wanted to appear, and he would have to redeem himself somewhat. It would be disastrous to lose face so completely. He began to speak flippantly about death: it wouldn't much bother him if he dropped dead at this very moment. But the funeral must be conducted according to his own wishes. He himself would make a bell to ring his knell, with the clapper made from the thighbone of an ass, because he had been such a fool. And the parson would deliver the briefest oration the world had ever heard, just setting his foot on the grave and saying: 'I declare you dead, to exist no more!'

But Olga was getting bored with all this and was rapidly losing her shyness. She was wearing a red silk ribbon at her neck which made her look quite ladylike — the pin was no longer in evidence.

He would have to try even harder, he thought to himself. 'I had hoped that this would come to something. My ex-fiancée at the Vicarage has so embroidered me with your initials that I'm a sight to see. There's Olga Rolandsen on virtually everything I own. I thought it was a sign from Heaven. But I'll be going now, and so say goodbye to you.'

With a flourish of his hat, he took his leave. His parting shot was masterful, at least. It would surely be odd if she didn't spend a little time thinking about him now!

What had actually happened? Even the sexton's daughter had rejected him. All right! But weren't there indications that it was all pretence? Why had she been sitting outside the door if she hadn't seen him approaching? And why had she dressed herself up with the red silk ribbon like a lady?

But Rolandsen's illusions were to be shattered only a few evenings later. He was at his window when he spotted Olga going to Mack's store. She stayed there late into the evening, and when she returned home she was accompanied by both Fredrik and Elise. Proud Rolandsen should have just kept cheerful and hummed a little tune or drummed nonchalantly with his fingers and continued thinking about his own affairs; instead, he made a big detour and came out on to the road again far ahead of the three of them. He paused to get his breath back, and then set off towards them.

They were taking an inordinately long time; Rolandsen could neither see nor hear them. He whistled and sang to himself as if they might be sitting somewhere in the forest watching him. At last he saw them coming, blatantly dawdling despite the lateness of the hour, when they should have been hurrying back to their respective homes. Chewing carelessly on a long stalk of grass and sporting a sprig of sallow in his buttonhole, the great Rolandsen approached the little group. The two men greeted one another as they met, and the ladies nodded.

'You look hot,' said Fredrik. 'Where have you been?'

'It's spring; I'm walking into the new season,' Rolandsen answered over his shoulder as he went by.

No nonsense, just total self-confidence! How slowly, casually and dispassionately he had walked past them. He had even had the strength to look Elise Mack up and down. But he was hardly out of their sight before he slipped into the forest again and no longer felt so superior, but defeated and distressed. Olga was unimportant now, and even as he thought of her he pulled the brooch from his pocket, broke it into pieces and threw it away. For now there was Mack's daughter Elise, tall and brown, with a flash of white teeth when she smiled. God had led her across his path. She had not said one word, and she would probably be going home again the next day. There was no hope whatsoever.

All right then.

But back home at the telegraph station Miss van Loos was waiting for him. He had reminded her already that the past was over and done with, that it would be best for her to leave the area. And she had said he need not ask her twice: Farewell for ever. But there she was again, waiting for him.

'Here's the tobacco pouch I promised you,' she said. 'If you're not too proud to take it.'

He did not take it, but retorted: 'A tobacco pouch? I never use pouches like that.'

'Oh, well,' she said, drawing back her hand.

He forced himself to mollify her once more: 'It can't be me you promised it to. Think again — perhaps it was the vicar. A married man!'

She did not perceive that the little joke had cost him an effort, and she could not refrain from saying: 'I saw the ladies along the road; I suppose it's them you've been chasing after.'

'And what's that got to do with you?'

'Ove!'

'Why don't you move away elsewhere? You can see that this is no good.'

'It would be all right if only you weren't such a peacock and wanted to flirt with all the women you see.'

'Are you trying to drive me completely out of my

mind?' he yelled. 'Goodnight!'

Miss van Loos called after him: 'Yes, you're a charming fellow! I've heard a thing or two about you!'

What was the point of spelling out the details? And anyway, wasn't a poor soul allowed to have a little genuine lovesickness to cope with on top of everything else? Without further ado, Rolandsen went up to his office, straight to the instrument, and asked one of the operators at the Rosengaard telegraph station to send him half a cask of cognac at the first opportunity. There was no sense in carrying on like this for ever.

# 7

Elise Mack spent rather more time than usual at the factory on this occasion. She had come over from the big house at Rosengaard solely to be of some comfort to her father during his visit; she would probably not have set foot in the village at all if she could have avoided it.

With the passing years Elise Mack was becoming more and more of a fine lady. Her dresses were red and white and yellow, and people were starting to address her as 'Ma'am' even though her father was neither a clergyman nor a doctor. She shone like a sun or a star above everyone else.

She went to the telegraph station with some telegrams, and was received by Rolandsen. He spoke only the few words that were needed, and did not make the mistake of nodding familiarly and asking how she was. In fact he made no mistakes of any kind.

'It says "ostrich feathers" twice here. I don't know whether that's deliberate?'

'Twice? Let me see. No, goodness, you're right. Could you lend me a pen?'

As she took off her glove to write, she went on: 'It's to a shopkeeper in town; he'd have really laughed at me. Is it right now?'

'Yes, it's all right now.'

'And you're still here,' she said, remaining seated. 'As you have been for years.'

Rolandsen must know what he was doing by not applying for promotion to a better posting. There must be something that held him here year after year.

'You have to be somewhere,' was all he said.

'Couldn't you come to Rosengaard? Wouldn't that be some improvement?'

A delicate blush suffused her cheeks—perhaps she would rather have left that unsaid.

'I wouldn't want such a big station.'

'No, I suppose you're still too young.'

He gave a wan smile. 'It's very kind of you anyway to assume that that's the reason.'

'If you came over to us, you'd find it's a bigger neighbourhood. The doctor's family next door, and the bookkeeper, and all the assistants from the store. And there are always interesting people from the boats.'

Like Captain Henriksen of the coastal steamer, Rolandsen thought to himself.

But what was the point of all this gracious

53

behaviour? Had Rolandsen suddenly become a different man from yesterday? He knew that he was completely and utterly without hope in his foolish love, and there was probably nothing more to be said. She gave him her hand as she went, omitting to put her glove on first. There was a rustle of silk as she swept down the steps.

Rolandsen sat down at his desk, a bent and shabby figure, and sent the telegrams. His breast was filled with a turmoil of strange emotions. The warmth of that velvety hand had penetrated right through him. Properly considered, perhaps his situation was not so wretched after all; the invention might bring in a significant sum of money if he could ever get hold of three hundred crowns. He was a bankrupt millionaire. But one day he would find a solution.

The curate's wife was the next to arrive, with a message to send to her father. Rolandsen's confidence had been bolstered by the previous visit; he no longer felt a good-for-nothing, but the equal of other great men. He chatted to her, just a few general words. She too stayed longer than was strictly necessary, and invited him to call at the Vicarage.

He met her again that evening, on the road below the telegraph station, and she didn't hurry past but stopped to talk. She could not have objected or she would not have lingered.

'So you play the guitar,' she said.

'Yes. If you wait a minute I'll show you how good I am.'

He went in to fetch the guitar.

The curate's wife waited. She couldn't have minded or she wouldn't have waited.

Rolandsen sang to her of his sweetheart and his one true love, and though the songs were nothing much, he had a beautiful strong voice. He had an ulterior motive in keeping her standing in the road: there was a possibility that someone might be taking a stroll at about that time. It had happened before. Even if the curate's wife had been in a hurry, it would have been difficult for her to get away now, and they went on talking again for quite a long time. He spoke in a completely different way from her husband, and it sounded as if he came from an entirely different part of the world; when he produced his most splendid phrases her eyes became big and round like those of an attentive child.

'Well, God be with you,' she said as she finally left him.

'I'm sure He is,' he replied.

She gave a start. 'Are you certain of that? How?'

'He has every reason to be. Obviously He's Lord over all Creation, but it can't be anything special to be a god of animals and mountains. It's really us human beings that make Him what He is. So why shouldn't He be with us?'

Having delivered this impressive speech, Rolandsen looked rather pleased with himself. The curate's wife would be puzzling over him as she walked home. Ha-ha, it was not so surprising that the little dome resting on his shoulders should have made such a great invention after all!

But now the cognac had arrived. Rolandsen had carried the cask up himself from the quay. He made no detours with his burden, but carried it openly under his strong arm in broad daylight. So emboldened was his heart. There followed a period of consolation in adversity. There were nights when he walked out and became the lord of the highways; he kept them clear of all strangers coming ashore in their lawful pursuit of the opposite sex.

One Sunday a boat's crew turned up at church, all of them somewhat the worse for drink. After the service they strolled about on the road instead of going back on board; they were quaffing bottles of aquavit and gradually became increasingly merry, much to the annoyance of passers-by. The curate had been out to the road and spoken to them, but without result. Then came the mayor, wearing his gold-braided cap. Some of them went on board, but three men, Big Ulrik among them, still refused to budge. They wanted everyone to know they were ashore, they insisted loudly, and the girls were all theirs. After all, they had Ulrik with them, and Ulrik was well-known from Lofoten to Finnmark. Come and do your worst!

Many of the villagers had gathered, further down the road or in among the trees of the forest, according to their degree of courage, all keen to see Big Ulrik as he swaggered about.

'I'm asking you to go aboard,' the mayor said.

'Otherwise I'll have to give you an official warning.'

'Go on home and take your cap with you!' yelled Ulrik.

The mayor wondered whether to seek help and get the madman tied up.

'You'd better not defy me when I'm wearing my cap of office,' he said.

Ulrik and his companions laughed so much at this that they nearly split their sides. One bold fisher-lad went past, and got head-butted and roughed up. 'Let's have the next!' bellowed Ulrik.

'A rope!' cried the mayor at the sight of blood. 'Run and fetch a rope, one of you. We must seize him.'

'You and who else?' Ulrik jeered, in a tone of invincibility. And his three companions nearly made themselves sick with laughter.

But now along the road came Big Rolandsen, walking slowly and easily, his eyes fixed straight ahead of him, following his usual route. He greeted the mayor and stopped.

'It's Rolandsen!' Ulrik cried. 'Look at Rolandsen, boys!'

The mayor said: 'He's gone completely crazy. He drew blood from one of our lads just now. Let's try and get a rope on him.'

'A rope?'

The mayor gave a nod. 'I won't tolerate this any longer.'

'There's no point in that,' said Rolandsen. 'What can you do with a rope? Let me have a go at him.'

Ulrik approached. He put out his hand to Rolandsen, but then suddenly delivered a punch. He obviously felt that he had come up against something firm and solid; he drew back, shouting: 'Good morning, Mr Rolandsen the telegraph-operator! I'll give you your name and profession so that you'll know who you are.'

Rolandsen made no immediate reaction, but he did not intend to let slip the chance for a fight. He was annoyed with himself for being so ridiculously slow to anger and for not having returned the first blow straight away. He would have to enter into a slanging match to keep things going. They exchanged insults and yelled like drunkards, boasting of what they would do to each other. When one dared the other to attack and threatened to give him a pummelling like a massage with olive oil, the other responded: 'Good, I'm ready for you; I'll lay my hands on you so gently you'll think you're being caressed by a woman!'

The crowd thought both parties were giving as good as they got. But the mayor could see Rolandsen's anger and satisfaction increasing by the minute—his lips wore a constant smile.

Then Ulrik clipped him under the nose, and Rolandsen's wrath was kindled at last. He shot out his fist, grabbed his assailant's coat, but failed to get a proper grip and it gave way. There was no point in ripping up a duffle coat. He leapt forward again with a scornful laugh, his teeth flashing white in a grin of pleasure. Now they would see some action!

When Ulrik tried a head-butt, Rolandsen realised that it was his opponent's speciality. But Rolandsen was master of another: the side of the open hand aimed in a long slow swing at the jawbone. The blow has to strike the side of the chin, and it sends an almighty shock-wave through the head, the brain spins and you crash to the ground. But nothing gets broken and there's no blood, apart from a trickle round the nose and mouth. You're more or less out for the count.

Suddenly Big Ulrik took a direct blow, and down he went, staggering quite a way before falling some distance beyond the edge of the road. His legs buckled and twisted under him as if he were dead. His head went into a whirl and he lost consciousness. Rolandsen was well enough versed in the parlance of the brawl to shout out: 'Let's have the next!' He looked thoroughly happy and did not even notice that his shirt was torn open at the collar.

The 'next' were Ulrik's two companions, now silent and thoughtful, no longer holding their sides in mirth.

'You're nothing but kids,' Rolandsen taunted scornfully. 'Do you want me to knock a few wrinkles into you?'

The mayor convinced the two men that they should see sense, however, and pick up their mate and help him to sanctuary on board their own ship. 'I'm very grateful to you,' he said to Rolandsen.

But as Rolandsen watched the three of them going off down the road, he felt far from satisfied, and yelled after them as they disappeared: 'Come back tomorrow night. Smash a window at the telegraph station and I'll get the message. Huh, you're nothing but children!'

As usual, he made a lot of it, boasting and bragging. But the audience was dispersing. Then a lady came over to Rolandsen and gazed at him with shining eyes, proffering her hand. It was the curate's wife. She too had been observing the events.

'You were really magnificent,' she said. 'He'll remember that.'

She could see that his shirt was ripped open. The sun had tanned a circle of brown around his neck, and below it he looked white and naked.

He fastened his shirt and greeted her. It was far from unwelcome to have such attention from the curate's wife in full view of everyone. The victor of the battle was elated, and could afford himself a friendly chat with this childlike creature. Poor woman, her shoes were cheap and shabby and she seemed to command little respect.

'It's a misuse of those eyes to look at me,' he said.

Her cheeks blushed red.

'Are you homesick for town life?' he asked.

'Oh, no,' she replied. 'I like it here too. But listen, why don't you come over and see us today?'

He thanked her but regretted that he could not. He had to go to the office on Sundays just as he did on Mondays. 'But thank you,' he said. 'There's one thing I envy the vicar,' he added, 'and that's you.'

'What . . .?'

'I don't mean to be rude, but I definitely envy him you.'

Well, he had done it now. It would be difficult to find anyone as good as he was at dispensing a little joy.

'What a one you are for a joke,' she responded when she had recovered from the shock.

Rolandsen, on his way home, thought that all in all it had been a good day. In the intoxication of his victory mood he began to think about how frequently the curate's young wife was beginning to chat to him. A streak of sly cunning began to manifest itself: perhaps she might be persuaded to discharge Miss van Loos, and so free him from his heavy fetters. He could hardly request it outright, but there were other ways. Maybe she would do him that little service now they were such good friends — who could tell?

# 8

The curate and his wife were startled out of sleep during the night by somebody singing. Nothing like that had ever happened to them before. The song seemed to be coming from the garden below. The sun was shining out over the world, the gulls had awoken, it was three o'clock in the morning.

'I think I can hear singing,' said the curate from his room.

'It's coming from outside my window,' his wife answered.

She listened. She recognised that crazy Rolandsen's voice and heard his guitar. He was completely reckless, singing of his only true love right below her window. She felt hot with embarrassment.

The curate came in and peered out of the window. 'It's Rolandsen, the telegraph-operator, by the look of things,' he said, with a frown. 'He's just had half a cask of brandy delivered. The man's a disgrace.'

But his wife was reluctant to see this little episode in such a black light. He was such a fascinating young man: he could fight like a stevedore and sing divinely. He brought variety into a monotonous life of trivial events.

'It's probably meant to be a serenade,' she said with a smile.

'Which you are hardly in a position to accept,' the curate retorted. 'Do you think?'

He would always find something to carp about! She sighed. 'Well, it's not that serious. It's only a bit of fun on his part.' But she resolved to herself never again to make eyes at Rolandsen and cause him to behave so foolishly.

'I don't believe it—he's starting to sing another one!' the curate exclaimed. He went over to the window just as he was, and knocked on the glass.

Rolandsen looked up. It was the vicar himself standing there, as large as life. The song died on his lips. He looked thoroughly crestfallen, stood for a moment in confusion, and then walked off out of the garden.

'Well,' said the curate, 'I've got rid of him.' He was by no means displeased to have achieved so much by simply showing himself. 'He'll get a letter from me in the morning,' he went on. 'I've had my eye on him for some time for his scandalous way of life.'

'Couldn't I just tell him that we don't want him singing here at night?'

The curate continued, without listening to his wife's suggestion: 'And then I'll go and talk to him!' He said this with emphasis, as if he expected that a talk with Rolandsen would produce wonderful results.

He returned to his room and lay down to think about the matter. He was no longer prepared to turn a blind eye to this dissolute lunatic whose arrogant affectations and way of life were such a disturbing influence on the village. The curate did not discriminate, but sent his letters out to all and sundry, incurring both fear and respect. He would lighten the darkness of his flock. He still remembered Levion's sister. She had not improved her ways, and the curate had been forced to dispense with the services of her brother as lay-helper. Ill-fortune had visited Levion: his wife had died. But the curate had confronted him even at the funeral. It was a hair-raising story. When the good man was about to go and bury his wife, he recalled having promised Fredrik Mack at the factory a slaughtered calf. He had to go in the same direction now, and the days were no longer cool enough to let the meat lie, so he took the carcase with him. The curate heard about it from Enoch, the piously humble Enoch with his chronic earache, and he sent for Levion at once.

'I cannot continue to retain you as a lay-helper,' said the curate. 'Your sister is living in a state of sin in your home, you're keeping a house of ill-repute — you even sleep in your bed at night while a man enters the premises.'

'Regrettably,' Levion replied, 'I have to admit it has

been known to occur.'

'And another thing. You take your wife to her grave and carry a dead calf along with her. How could you possibly do such a thing?'

But Levion, the simple fisherman-farmer, stared at the curate uncomprehendingly and found the criticism meaningless. His late wife had been a thrifty soul and would have been the first to remind him to take the calf along, if she had been able to. 'You're going the same way,' his dear departed would have said.

'If you insist on being so fussy and particular, you'll never get a capable helper,' he said eventually.

'That's my problem,' the curate replied. 'But you can consider yourself dismissed.'

Levion looked down at his sou'wester. He had undeniably suffered a disgrace, and his neighbours would gloat over his fall.

The curate's indignation did not abate. 'For heaven's sake,' he said, 'can't you get your sister to marry the man?'

'Do you think I haven't tried?' said Levion. 'But she's not quite sure who it is.'

The curate stood open-mouthed. 'Not quite what?' And as it sank in, he wrung his hands. Then, with a curt nod: 'Well, as I said, I'll get another helper.'

'Who will it be?'

'There's no reason why I should tell you. But it's to be Enoch.'

Levion pondered this information for a while. He knew that man, he still had things to settle with him.

65

'So it's Enoch,' was all he said, and off he went.

Enoch would be good at the job. He was a deep man, meticulous and solid, without any affectations. It was rumoured that he was an unreliable companion at sea; many years ago, so the tale went, he had been caught pulling up other people's lines. But that was probably just envy and slander. There was nothing distinguished about his appearance, and the scarf around his ears was hardly an elegant touch. And when he encountered anyone on the road, he was wont to press his finger first on one nostril and then on the other and blow through each in turn. But God did not pay attention to external appearances, and His humble servant Enoch probably had the praiseworthy intention of smartening himself up before he met people. As he drew near, he would say 'Peace be unto you!', and when he took his leave, 'Go in peace!' Everything he did was meticulous and deliberate. He even seemed to wear the big sheath knife, which hung from his belt, with a grateful attitude, as if to say that he recognised that there were many unfortunates who did not even have a knife to cut with. At the last church offering Enoch had attracted attention with the size of his gift, putting a note on the collection plate. Had he really earned so much money lately? Some higher power must have added its mite to his savings. He owed nothing to Mack's store, his dried fish was still untouched, his family was adequately clothed. And his house was a model of propriety. He had one son, a fine example of good behaviour and decorum. The boy had been out with the fishing fleet in the Lofoten Islands and so had the right to come home with a blue anchor tattooed on his hand, but he did not. His father had taught him humility and the fear of God at an early age. To go about meekly and quietly brought the blessing of the Lord, that was Enoch's view . . .

While the curate lay thinking, the morning wore on. That wretch Rolandsen had ruined his night's sleep, and at six he got up. He discovered that his wife had quietly dressed and was already out.

Later that morning the curate's wife went to see Rolandsen and said: 'You mustn't come singing here at night.'

'I know I behaved stupidly,' he said. 'I had expected to find Miss van Loos there, but she must have moved.'

'So you were serenading her?'

'Yes, just a little snatch of song to welcome the morning.'

'Actually, it was my room,' she said.

'Miss van Loos used to sleep there before, in the old vicar's time.'

The curate's wife had no more to say, her eyes had lost their sparkle.

'Well, thank you very much,' she said as she turned to go. 'It was nice to listen to, but don't do it again.'

'I promise. If I'd known . . . Of course I wouldn't have presumed . . .' Rolandsen looked as if he would like to sink into the ground.

When the curate's wife got home, she said: 'I'm

really very sleepy today.'

'Is it any wonder?' her husband replied. 'You could hardly sleep for that loudmouth outside.'

'I think it would be best if Miss van Loos went,' she said.

'Miss van Loos?'

'He's engaged to her. We'll probably never get any peace at nights.'

'He shall have a letter from me today.'

'It would be simplest if Miss van Loos left.'

The curate thought to himself that this was far from being the simplest way, since it would cause him extra expense for a new housekeeper. Besides, Miss van Loos was very capable and hard-working; without her, there would be no order at all. He remembered how it had been when they first got married and his wife was managing the house herself — indeed, he would never forget it.

'Who would you want to replace her?' he asked.

'I would rather do her work myself.'

The curate gave a bitter laugh. 'Yes, it would really get done then.'

His wife was hurt and offended, exclaiming: 'It seems to me that I have to be involved in running my own house all the time anyway. So what the house-keeper does isn't any great help.'

The curate was silent. There was no point in further argument, God help him! 'We can't ask her to go,' he said. But there sat his wife with her shoes so split that it was a lamentable sight. As he went out he said:

'We'll have to see if we can get you a new pair of shoes
fairly soon.'

'Oh, well, it's summer now,' she replied.

# 9

The last of the fishing boats were ready to sail; the season was over. But the sea was still full of herring, they had been sighted along the coast, and the prices had fallen. Mack had bought up all the herring he could get, and no one had heard of any delays in his payments. Only with the last boat had he asked for a little time while he telegraphed south for money. But immediately there had been gossip: Aha—he's in difficulties!

But Mack was as supreme as ever. In the midst of all his other business activities he had promised the curate's wife a bakery—fine, the bakery was progressing, the workmen had started, the foundations were laid. She found it a real pleasure to go and see her bakery taking shape. Now the actual building had to be constructed, and for that Mack needed different workmen. They too had been sent for by telegraph, said Mack.

But the baker at the mayor's house had pulled himself together. What the curate's letter had failed to achieve, Mack had accomplished with his foundation walls. 'If it's bread they want, bread they shall have,' said the baker. But everyone could see that the poor man was just flailing helplessly around, and was about to be put out of business by Mack.

Rolandsen was sitting in his room drawing up a remarkable announcement over his own signature. He read it several times and found it in order. He put it in his pocket, picked up his hat and went out. He took the road down towards Mack's office at the factory.

He had been expecting Miss van Loos to leave; but she had not. The curate's wife had evidently not dismissed her. Rolandsen had miscalculated when he hoped that she would do him that favour. He came to his senses again. In future he would keep his feet on the ground; he obviously had not made such an impression as he had thought.

He had, however, received a letter from the curate of serious and censorious content. Rolandsen did not try to conceal what had befallen him, he admitted it to everyone. The letter was well-deserved, he said, and had done him good. No clergyman had bothered with him since he was confirmed. He was even tempted to suggest that the curate ought to send out lots of letters like that, for the benefit and edification of all.

But no one could detect in Rolandsen any such

71

beneficial effects recently. On the contrary, he looked more troubled and pensive then ever, and seemed to be grappling with one particular idea. Shall I do it or shall I not? he seemed to be muttering. And now that his former fiancée Miss van Loos had accosted him first thing that morning and pestered him again about the foolish serenade at the Vicarage, he had left her with the ominous words 'I shall do it!'

He walked into Mack's office and said good morning. He was completely sober. Father and son were standing writing, one at either side of the desk. Old Mack offered him a seat, but Rolandsen would not sit.

'All I wanted to say was that I was the one who broke into your office.'

Father and son both stared at him.

'I've come to give myself up,' said Rolandsen. 'It wouldn't be right for me to keep quiet any longer, it's bad enough already.'

'Leave us alone for a bit,' Old Mack said.

Fredrik went out.

Mack asked: 'Are you in your right mind today?'

'I was the one who did it,' Rolandsen shouted—his voice was designed as much for ranting as for singing.

A few moments passed in silence. Mack blinked his eyes a few times while he thought about it. 'So you were the one who did it, you say?'

'Yes.'

Mack carried on thinking. His good brain had solved more than one problem in its day; he was used to weighing matters up quickly.

'Will you still be of the same mind tomorrow?'

'Yes. From now on I won't try to hide the deed. I've had a letter from the vicar, that's what's changed me.'

Was Mack starting to believe him now? Or was it just for the sake of form that he went along with it?

'When did you do the break-in?'

Rolandsen named the night.

'How did you go about it?'

Rolandsen described his actions in detail.

'There were some papers in the box with the money. Did you see them?'

'Yes, there were some papers.'

'You took one with you. Where is it?'

'I haven't got it. A paper? No.'

'It was my life insurance policy.'

'A life insurance policy, yes, now I remember. I have to admit that I burned it.'

'Well, that was very wrong of you. You caused me a lot of trouble getting another one.'

'I was so confused, I couldn't think straight. I beg you to forgive the whole affair.'

'There was another box with several thousand crowns in, why didn't you take that?'

'I didn't find it.'

Mack had finished weighing things up. Whether Rolandsen had committed the felony or not, he was the most wonderful burglar he could have had. He would certainly not keep quiet about the matter, but would broadcast it to every person he met. The last fishing boats would take the news with them to all the

73

traders along the coast. Mack felt himself saved.

'I've never heard anything before about you going around and . . . about your having this weakness,' he said.

To which Rolandsen replied that no, he didn't; he didn't rob nest-eggs. He went to the bank itself.

That was a good one for Mack! He merely said in reproach: 'But to do it to *me* . . .!'

'I was drunk at the time. I'd made myself over-confident and didn't know what I was doing.'

There was not much room for any more doubt that the confession was true. The crazy telegraph-operator lived a wild life and did not earn a great deal. And the brandy from Rosengaard was pretty expensive.

'I'm sorry to say I've got more to confess,' went on Rolandsen. 'I haven't got the money to give back to you.'

Mack showed no concern. 'That's not important,' he said. 'What upsets me is all the nasty gossip it's involved me in. All the affronts to me and my family.'

'I was thinking of doing something about that.'

'What would that be?'

'I was going to take down your notice from the Vicar-age gatepost and put up one of my own instead.'

There was Rolandsen's impulsiveness again. 'No, I'm not asking you to do that,' said Mack. 'It will be hard enough for you anyway, you poor chap. But I'd like you to write a declaration here.' He nodded towards Fredrik's place at the desk.

While Rolandsen was writing, Mack sat in thought.

The whole serious affair was now turning out for the good. It would cost something, but it would be money well spent, because his renown would travel the length and breadth of the land.

Mack read the declaration through and said: 'Yes, that's fine. I don't intend to make use of it, of course.'

'It's in your hands,' said Rolandsen.

'Nor do I intend to mention this interview. It will remain between the two of us.'

'Then I'll tell everyone myself,' said Rolandsen. 'The vicar's letter was quite explicit that I should make a public confession.'

Mack opened his fireproof safe, and took out a wad of notes. He had the chance now to show what kind of man he was. And nobody would know that one of the fishing boats down in the bay was waiting for just this sum of money before sailing home.

Mack counted out four hundred crowns and said: 'I don't want to insult you, but I'm in the habit of keeping my word. I promised four hundred crowns, and now they're yours.'

Rolandsen went towards the door. 'I deserve your contempt,' he said.

'My contempt!' exclaimed Mack. 'Let me tell you something . . .'

'I'm filled with remorse at your generosity. You're not even demanding to have me punished. You're rewarding me.'

But it was no big thing for Mack to lose two hundred crowns in a burglary. It was only when he had rewarded the thief with double that amount that the entire affair would reflect any real glory. 'You are an unfortunate man now, Rolandsen. You'll lose your job. I won't miss this money, but it may be of practical use to you in the short term. You think it over.'

'I can't take it,' said Rolandsen.

Mack picked up the notes and stuffed them into Rolandsen's pocket.

'Let it be a loan, then,' said Rolandsen.

The generous and lordly merchant went along with that and replied: 'All right. A loan.' But he knew full well that he would never see the money again.

Rolandsen had a crushed look, as if he were now bearing the heaviest burden of his life. It was pitiful to see.

'Now hurry up and get back on the straight and narrow!' said Mack encouragingly. 'One mistake isn't irredeemable.'

Rolandsen thanked him most humbly for everything, and left.

'I'm a thief,' he said to the factory girls as he passed them. He confessed the whole thing.

He went on down to the Vicarage gate. He tore off Mack's notice and put up his own in its place. It stated that he, and he alone, was the thief. And the next day was Sunday: many churchgoers would pass that very spot.

# 10

Rolandsen seemed to be behaving sensibly again. After his notice had been read by everyone in the village, he kept himself to himself and avoided meeting people. This made a conciliatory impression; at least the fallen man had changed his outlook and was not persisting in his immoral ways. But the truth was that Rolandsen had no time to wander about the roads now; he was busily occupied in his room every night. He had put his samples in medicine bottles of all shapes and sizes that he now had to pack into boxes and send off by post to every part of the country. And he was at the telegraph instrument both early and late. He wanted to get things finished before he was dismissed.

Rolandsen's scandal also became known at the Vicarage, of course, and great was the sympathy towards

Miss van Loos for having been engaged to such a man. The curate ushered her into his study and had a lengthy and kind-hearted talk with her.

Miss van Loos was now very definitely disinclined to continue her attachment to Rolandsen; she would go to him and confirm that it was over.

She found him abject and depressed, but she was unmoved. 'Fine things you've been up to,' she said.

'I was hoping you'd come, so that I could ask you to forgive me.'

'Forgive you? Now I've heard everything! Let me tell you, Ove, that I'm completely at a loss to understand you. And I really don't want to have anything more to do with you on this earth. Nobody can call me a thief or a rogue, I just go about my honest business. Haven't I warned you to the best of my ability? And it's made no difference at all to you. An engaged man making himself available to other women, like an expensive jewel? And afterwards you steal money from people and then confess publicly on a gatepost. I feel so ashamed I can hardly contain myself and don't know what to do. You hold your tongue! I know you, all you want to do is look big and be one of the boys. My love for you has been open and sincere, but you've been like a leper and sullied my whole life with this burglary. There's no point your trying to speak. My God, everyone says the same, that you've deceived me and abused me. The vicar says I should leave you and go away, however much he needs me. Don't just stand there trying to hide, Ove. You're a sinner in the sight of

God and man, and nothing but scum. And if I still call you Ove, I don't mean it and you needn't think that I want to make things up with you. As far as I'm concerned we're no longer friends nor even acquaintances. No one could have done more for you than I have, I'm sure of that. But you've just been totally irresponsible towards me and taken advantage of me from start to finish. Though I'm sorry to say it must be partly my fault, because I've turned a blind eye up till now and let you get away with it.'

The wretched man stood there quite unable to defend himself. He had never heard her in such a frenzy before. His gross misdemeanour had completely shaken her. When she finally came to a halt she seemed utterly exhausted.

'I'll mend my ways,' he said.

'You? Mend your ways?' she replied with a bitter laugh. 'There's no point in that any more. You can't undo what's done, and I don't want my character stained by you—I come from a respectable family. I'm telling you straight: I'm leaving the day after tomorrow on the post-boat. But I don't want you coming to the quay to see me off, and the vicar agrees. I'm saying goodbye to you today—for ever. Thanks for the good times we've had together. I don't want to remember the bad.'

She turned decisively and strode off. But then she added: 'You can stay in the woods above the quay if you like, and wave from there. I don't care one way or the other.'

'Give me your hand,' he said.

'No, I won't. You know only too well yourself what your hand is guilty of.'

Rolandsen bent his head low. 'Can't we write to one another?' he asked. 'Just a few words from time to time?'

'I won't write. Never. You've made jokes so often about it all being over, but now I'm suddenly good enough again. Well, now I know everything's a lie! I hope you get on all right. You can reach me at my father's address in Bergen if you want to write. But I'm not asking you to.'

As Rolandsen climbed the stairs to his room, he had a distinct feeling that the engagement was definitely off. It was strange, he thought, that he had been talking with her outside only seconds before.

It was a busy day for him, he had to pack the last of his samples and get them off by the post-boat the day after next, then gather his belongings together and have them ready for his removal. The all-powerful Inspector of Telegraphs was on his way.

It went without saying that he would be summarily dismissed. There were no complaints about his work, and Mack, despite his influence, would probably not seek retribution; but justice had to be seen to be done.

The meadows were covered in grass now, and the forests were in leaf; the mild nights were here again. The bay was empty, all the boats had gone, and Mack's ships had sailed south with their cargoes of herring. It was summer.

In this warm and brilliant season, the church was well attended on Sundays. By land and sea crowds of people came, including skippers from Bergen and Haugesund who were at anchor along the coast drying their fish on the rocks. They came regularly year after year, growing old in the place. They socialised at church in their finest clothes, in coloured calico shirts and watch-chains of finest hair; one even wore gold earrings, which brightened up the congregation. But the dry conditions also gave rise to a dreadful forest fire further up the fjords, so the summer weather had its disadvantages.

Enoch had taken up office and was now the curate's solemn and conscientious lay-helper, still with his scarf round his ears. The younger folk were amused at the sight, but the older members of the congregation were angry at seeing the door of the choirstall desecrated by such a monkey, and they lodged a complaint with the curate. Could Enoch not stuff cotton wool in his ears? But Enoch told the curate that he could not do without the scarf, because of the pain that penetrated his whole head. This caused his predecessor, Levion, to burst into malicious laughter at Enoch and to express his amazement that he could wear such a scarf round his head in the middle of the day in such heat.

Ever since his humiliating dismissal, the villainous Levion, full of spite and envy, had not stopped perse-cuting his successor. Whenever he went out spearing flounder at night, he would position himself on Enoch's bit of coast and hunt for the fish nearest to

Enoch. And if he needed a rowlock or a baler, he would
seek it in Enoch's wood down by the shore. He never
let Enoch of his sight . . .

The rumour soon went round that Miss van Loos
had broken off her engagement and was about to leave
the Vicarage because of the shame and disgrace. Mack
felt sorry for the dishonoured telegraph-operator and
determined to make at least an attempt to heal the rift.
He took Rolandsen's confession off the gatepost himself, and declared that it had been put there against his
wishes. He then went down to the Vicarage. Mack
could afford to be benevolent, he was already aware of
the profound impact his treatment of the offender had
made. Everyone greeted him again now as before,
perhaps with even more respect than in the old days.
There was only one Mack on the entire coast, after all!

But his visit to the Vicarage was to no avail. Miss van
Loos was moved to tears by the fact that Mack himself
had come. But no one would persuade her to make it
up with Rolandsen, never in all the world. Mack got
the impression that it was the curate who had made
her so determined.

When the housekeeper made her way down to the
quay, the curate and his wife accompanied her. They
both wished her a safe journey and saw her on to the
boat.

'Oh, heavens, I'm sure he's up there in the forest,
full of remorse,' cried Miss van Loos, taking out her
handkerchief.

The boat moved off, slipping away from its moorings with long smooth strokes of the oars.

'I can see him!' she shrieked, half standing up. She looked as if she was about to leap into the water and wade ashore. But then she started waving with all her might towards the forest. Until the boat disappeared round the point.

Rolandsen walked home through the forest as he had lately taken to doing; but when he found himself above the Vicarage gate he made his way down to the road again and followed it. All his samples of fish-glue had been despatched; he just had to await the results. It would not be long now. He clicked his fingers as he walked along, in cheerful spirits once more.

A little further on was Olga the sexton's daughter, sitting on a rock by the side of the road. What was she doing there? Rolandsen thought she was probably on her way back from the store and waiting for someone. Moments later she was joined by Elise Mack. Well, well, had the two become inseparable? She also sat down and seemed to be waiting. I'll delight the ladies by being humble and keeping out of their way, Rolandsen thought to himself. He turned quickly off into the forest. But the dry twigs cracked underfoot and they would be able to hear his steps; it was a pointless exercise and he gave up. It will have to be the road again, he thought, no need to delight them that much. So he returned to the road.

But it was not so easy to come face to face with Elise Mack. His heart began to pound, a wave of heat flowed through him and he paused. He had achieved nothing last time, and now there was the crime to consider. He withdrew into the forest once more. If only he could get past this clearing the dry twigs would end and the heather begin. He leaped through the clearing in a few huge bounds, and was saved. Suddenly he stopped. What the deuce was he jumping about like this for? Was he not Ove Rolandsen? He walked back defiantly into the clearing, snapping twigs with gay abandon.

When he at last regained the road, he saw the ladies still sitting in the same place. They were talking, and Elise was poking holes in the road with her parasol. Rolandsen stopped again. There is no one more cautious than a dare-devil. I'm a thief, he thought; how can I have the cheek to show myself? Shall I greet them and force them to acknowledge me? And as before he drew back into the trees. He was a great fool to go around with such feelings; he had plenty of other things to think about. In a few months' time he would be a gentleman of means — let there be no thought of love! He continued on his way.

He wondered if they were still sitting there. He turned and peered behind him. Fredrik had joined them now, and all three were walking towards him. He hurried off again with his heart in his mouth. With luck they hadn't seen him! They halted, and he heard Fredrik say: 'Listen! I think I can hear someone in the forest.' 'It's probably nothing at all,' Elise replied.

She might have said that precisely because she had seen him. The thought made him feel cold and bitter. Of course he was nothing — as yet. But wait another two months! What was she herself? A Virgin Mary, hard as iron, daughter of the well-known Lutheran, Mack of Rosengaard. Good luck to her!

There was a weathercock on the roof of the telegraph station on an iron pole. When Rolandsen got home, he climbed up on to the roof and gave the pole a blow with his own hands. The cock reeled backwards, and looked as if it were crowing. That was how it should look. It was very apt that the cock should crow.

# 11

And now came a time of lazy days for everyone—just a little inshore fishing on warm summer nights for the pleasure of it. Corn and potatoes growing and the long grass in the meadows, herring in every store-shed, cows and goats filling the pails full with milk and fattening themselves up.

Mack and his daughter Elise had gone home again; Fredrik was in charge of the factory and the store. But Fredrik's management was somewhat poor, he was obsessed by his love of the sea and hardly able to bear his landlubber's life. Captain Henriksen of the coastal steamer had half promised to find him a berth as mate on his ship, but nothing seemed to come of it. Perhaps Old Mack might buy his son a ship of his own? He seemed willing and often talked of it, but Fredrik had a feeling it would not come about. Fredrik had a pretty good awareness of the situation. He was not really a sailor by temperament at all, he was a cautious and reliable youth who did just enough in his daily life to get by. He took after his mother and was not a true Mack at all. But that was the way to be if you wanted to succeed in life: not do too much, but rather do slightly too little of everything, and it would be regarded as adequate. Look what had happened to Rolandsen, that reckless madman, with his excesses. He had turned into a common thief among his fellows, and had finally even lost his job. There he was now with this great weight on his conscience, wearing his clothes quite threadbare, and he had nowhere to live but a little room in Børre's house. That was where Ove Rolandsen had ended up. Børre was all right in his way, but he was the poorest and most wretched person in the village, with less herring in his store than anybody else. And as his daughter Pernilla was frail and sickly, his house was held in fairly low esteem. No decent man would live there.

It was rumoured that had Rolandsen presented himself a little more contritely to the Inspector he might perhaps have been able to keep his job. But he had simply assumed that he would be dismissed, and the Inspector had thus had no excuse to pardon him. And Old Mack, who might have acted as mediator, was not there.

But the curate was not entirely displeased with Rolandsen. 'I've heard that he drinks less than he used to,' he said, 'and I don't regard him as a completely hopeless case. He admits himself that it was because of a letter from me that he confessed to the burglary. One sometimes has a little satisfaction from one's efforts.'

Midsummer Eve came, bonfires were lit on the hilltops, and all the young people throughout the whole fishing community gathered round them, to the sound of accordions and fiddles. It was best to have almost no flames, but lots of smoke; when damp moss and juniper twigs were thrown on, the smoke was thickest and most aromatic.

Rolandsen's feeling of shame was still insufficient to keep him away from this popular festivity, and he sat on a hill playing his guitar and singing so loud that it echoed across the valley. When he came down to the bonfire it was obvious that he was as drunk as a lord and full of scintillating phrases. He was still his old self.

But then Olga the sexton's daughter came walking along the road below. It was far from her intention to stop, she was just on her way past. She might well have taken a different route, but she was young, and the accordion music attracted her. Her nostrils quivered and happiness surged within her; she was in love. She had been to the store earlier that day and Fredrik Mack had said enough for her to understand him, even though he had spoken cautiously. He too might be out for a stroll this evening.

She met the curate's wife and they walked along together, talking of none other than Fredrik Mack. He was the squire of the village, and even the curate's wife was secretly enamoured of him. He was so respectable and careful and had both feet firmly on the ground. She eventually noticed that Olga was being very bashful, so she asked: 'You're so quiet, my dear, don't tell me you're in love with young Mack?'

'Yes,' whispered Olga, and burst into tears.

The curate's wife stopped dead in her tracks. 'Olga, Olga! Does he care about you, too?'

'I think so.'

The curate's wife's eyes became blank and empty again and she stared into space. 'Well, well,' she said with a smile, 'God bless you, it will be all right, you'll see!' And she was even more friendly towards Olga.

When they reached the Vicarage, the curate was rushing up and down in consternation. 'There's a forest fire!' he cried. 'I saw it from my window!' He was gathering together axes and picks and men for his boat at the jetty. The fire was in Enoch's wood.

But Levion was there before the curate and his men. He was rowing back home from fishing as usual opposite Enoch's wood, with a nice little catch, when he suddenly glimpsed a small bright flame flickering among the trees and getting bigger and bigger. He nodded to himself, as if he knew what it might mean. But he could see a lot of activity on the Vicarage jetty and realised that help was on its way. He turned his boat immediately and rowed back to be first on the spot. It was an admirable trait in his character that he was willing to forget old grudges and hurry to his enemy's aid.

He put ashore and went up into the wood; he could hear the fire raging. He took his time, looking around carefully at every step. Suddenly he caught sight of Enoch dashing along in great haste. He was overcome by a feeling of curiosity, and concealed himself behind a rocky outcrop to keep watch. Enoch was drawing nearer, intent on his purpose, looking neither to right nor left, just rushing straight ahead. Had he discovered the presence of his antagonist, and was he seeking him out? When he was quite close Levion gave a yell. Enoch pulled up with a jerk. In his confusion, he smiled and said:

'The wood's on fire! Calamity has struck.'

Levion summoned up his courage and replied: 'It must be the hand of God.'

Enoch furrowed his brow. 'What are you doing here?' he asked.

All Levion's hatred flared up as he taunted him: 'Ha-ha! It'll be even hotter in your headscarf now!'

'Clear off!' Enoch shouted. 'It was probably you who started the fire!'

But Levion was blind and deaf to his threats. Enoch seemed to be heading directly for the rock where he was standing.

'You'd better watch out!' Levion cried. 'I've already torn off one of your ears — I can easily have the other!'

'Get out of here, I tell you,' Enoch replied, coming nearer.

Levion was choking with rage. 'Do you remember that day on the fjord? When you were pulling up my lines? And I pulled your ear off?'

So that was why Enoch always wore a scarf round his head: he only had one ear. These two neighbours had long been at one another's mercy and both had equally good reason to keep quiet about the whole episode.

'You're as good as a murderer,' said Enoch.

They could hear the curate's boat racing towards the shore, and the roar of the fast-approaching fire on the other side of them. Enoch twisted and turned, trying to frighten off Levion, threatening him with his sheath knife, that magnificent blade he was now armed with.

Levion rolled his eyes and shouted: 'Before you use the knife on me you might like to know there are people right behind me. Here they come!'

Enoch put the knife away again. 'Why are you standing there, anyway? Get out!'

'And what exactly are you doing here yourself?'

'That's nothing to do with you. I had to fetch something I'd hidden here. The fire's getting closer.'

But Levion refused to budge an inch, just to be awkward. The curate was almost up to them and must have been able to hear the quarrel from afar, but why should Levion care about him any more!

The boat was made fast, all the men came running up with their axes and picks. The curate gave a hasty word of greeting, to which he added: 'These Midsummer bonfires are a dangerous business, Enoch. The sparks fly in all directions. Where shall we start?'

Enoch stood in bewilderment; the curate seized him and pulled him away so that he could not continue his row with Levion.

'Which way's the wind blowing?' the curate asked. 'Come and show us where to dig a ditch.'

But Enoch looked as if he were standing on a bed of nails; trying to keep one eye on Levion, he just answered at random.

'Don't let this bit of bad luck upset you so much,' said the curate. 'Pull yourself together. We must put the fire out!' He took Enoch by the arm.

Some of the men went towards the fire and began digging. Levion still stood where he was, breathing heavily. He kicked at a stone lying near the rocky crag. He won't have hidden anything here, he thought, looking down—that was just a lie. Where he had kicked away some of the earth beneath the stone, a scarf came into view. The scarf belonged to Enoch, it was a discarded ear-protector. Levion picked it up, and could feel that it contained a package. He unwound the scarf—there was money inside, a lot of money, banknotes. And a large white document. He was immediately intrigued, and the thought of the stolen money came to mind as he unfolded the paper and tried to read it.

At that moment Enoch noticed what he was doing, and uttered a hoarse cry, tearing himself away from the curate and racing back towards Levion brandishing his sheath knife.

'Enoch! Enoch!' the curate exclaimed, trying to intercept him.

'This is the thief!' Levion yelled out to them all.

The curate thought Enoch must be so shocked by the fire that he had lost control of himself. 'Put your knife away!' he shouted.

Levion persisted: 'Here's Mack's burglar!'

'What do you mean?' asked the curate, uncomprehendingly.

Enoch rushed up to his opponent and tried to grab the package.

'I'm going to give it to the vicar!' Levion yelled. 'He'll see what kind of helper he has.'

Enoch sank down against a tree. His face was grey. The curate could not grasp the significance of the bank-notes, the scarf and the document.

'I found it there,' said Levion, his whole body trembling. 'He'd hidden it under a rock. Mack's name is on the paper.'

The curate began to read it, with growing astonishment. He looked up at Enoch and said: 'This is the insurance policy Mack lost, isn't it?'

'It's also the money he lost,' Levion responded.

Enoch straightened himself up. 'Then you must have put it there.'

The roar of the burning forest was getting closer, the heat was increasing all around them, but the three men just stood there.

'I don't know anything about it,' Enoch repeated. 'It must be Levion's idea of doing me a good turn.'

Levion retorted: 'There are two hundred crowns here—have I ever had as much as that? And isn't the scarf yours? Haven't you worn one like that round your ears?'

'Yes, you have, haven't you?' the curate interjected.

Enoch was silent.

The curate counted the notes. 'There isn't two hundred here,' he said.

'He's spent some,' said Levion.

Enoch stood there panting, but said in a firm and steady voice: 'I don't know anything about it. But you can be sure I'll remember you for this, Levion!'

The curate's mind was in a whirl. If Enoch was the thief, then Rolandsen had just been making a mockery of the letter of admonition he had been sent. But why would he have done that?

The heat was now becoming too intense and the three men made their way hastily down to the shore with the fire in pursuit. They had to get into the boat, and they had to push away from land.

'It's definitely Mack's policy, anyway,' said the curate. 'We'll have to report the matter. Row us back, Levion.'

Enoch had subsided into a silence and just sat staring straight ahead. 'Yes, let's go and report it,' he said, 'that's all I want.'

'Is it?' the curate replied with a heavy heart. And he closed his eyes involuntarily at the horror of the whole situation.

Enoch, in his greed, had been too naive. He had carefully secreted this to him unintelligible insurance document. It had a lot of stamps on it, and mentioned a large sum of money; he might eventually be able to

take it somewhere and dispose of it to advantage. He
certainly could not afford to throw it away.

The curate looked back at the fire. The men were
hard at work in the forest, trees were being felled, and
the darker gash of a broad trench was appearing. Rein-
forcements had arrived.

'The fire will burn itself out,' said Levion.

'Do you think so?'

'When it reaches the birch trees, it'll die down.'

And the boat with its three occupants made its way
round into the bay where the mayor's house stood.

# 12

When the curate came home that evening he had been weeping. There was so much deplorable sinfulness all round him. He was humbled and hurt and grieved; now his wife would not even get the shoes she so badly needed. Enoch's generous offering at the altar would have to he handed back, it was stolen money. And once again the curate would be penniless.

He went up to see his wife straight away. As soon as he reached the door he felt a surge of fury and despair. His wife was sewing. There were clothes all over the floor, a fork and a dishcloth from the kitchen on the bed, along with newspapers and crochet work. One of her slippers lay on the table. On the chest of drawers was a birch twig in leaf and a large pebble.

The curate started picking things up and tidying away, as was his wont.

'You needn't do that,' she said. 'I was going to put my slipper away as soon as I'd finished sewing.'

'But how can you sit in this mess and sew!'

She was offended at that and made no reply.

'What's the stone for?'

'It isn't *for* anything. I found it down on the beach and thought it looked so pretty.'

He picked up a little heap of dried grass lying on the dressing table and rolled it up in a newspaper.

'Perhaps you're keeping this for something too?' he asked, pausing for a moment.

'No, it's too old. It's sorrel, I was keeping it for a salad.'

'It's been here for over a week,' he said. 'It's left a stain on the polished surface.'

'There you are! No one should have polished furniture, you can't use it for anything.'

The curate gave a caustic laugh. His wife threw down her sewing and stood up.

He never left her in peace, he was always tormenting her with his idiocies. And so there developed another of those stupid and pointless arguments that they had repeated at regular intervals through the four years of their marriage. The curate had come up in all humility to beg his wife's patience about the shoes, but it became increasingly impossible to carry out his intention as his anger got the better of him. Everything was chaotic in the Vicarage now Miss van Loos had gone and his wife had taken over the housekeeping herself.

'And while we're on the subject, couldn't you try to be a bit more sensible about things in the kitchen?' he said.

'Sensible? I think I am being sensible. Is it any worse now than it was before?'

'I found the waste bin full of food yesterday.'

'It would be a lot better if you weren't always sticking your nose into everything.'

'I found a whole dish of gruel left over from dinner the other day.'

'Well, the maids had been at it and I couldn't serve it up any more.'

'I also found some rice pudding.'

'The milk had curdled. I couldn't help it.'

'And one day I found a boiled egg in the waste bin that had already been shelled.'

His wife was silent. But even on this charge she could have thought of something to say in self-justification.

'We're not at all well off,' said the curate, 'and you know we have to pay for the eggs. One day you even gave the cat an omelette.'

'Only a bit left over from dinner. You're being totally unreasonable, in my opinion; you ought to go to the doctor about that temper of yours.'

'I've seen you standing with the cat on your arm, holding a saucer of milk under its nose. And you do it in full view of the maids. They laugh at you behind your back.'

'They don't laugh at all. It's just you who's allowing

your bad temper to get the better of you.'

At length the curate went back down to his study. And his wife was finally left in peace.

At the breakfast table the next morning no one would have known from her appearance that she had suffered or been miserable. All her worries seemed to have melted away, and it was as if their quarrel had never taken place. Her happy and capricious nature was a great comfort to her and enabled her to cope with life. The curate's heart was touched again, and he wished he had kept quiet about these domestic issues — after all, the new housekeeper they were going to have was already on her way north.

'I'm sorry, you won't be able to have your new shoes now,' he said.

'No, no,' was all she said.

'I'll have to give back the offering Enoch made. He had stolen the money.'

'Really?'

'Yes — can you believe he was the one who broke into Mack's office? I reported him to the mayor yesterday.' The curate told her the whole story.

'So it wasn't Rolandsen after all,' she said.

'Him, that joker! A pitiful wretch! . . . But I'm afraid you'll have to wait for your shoes.'

'Oh, well, it doesn't matter.'

She was always like that, kind and self-sacrificing in the extreme, like a child. And the curate had never once heard her complain about their poverty.

'If only you could wear my shoes,' he said, his heart

warming to her again.

That really made her laugh. 'Yes—and you could wear mine. Ha-ha-ha!' So saying, she inadvertently knocked his plate off the table and it smashed, a cold cutlet landing on the floor with it. 'Wait a minute, I'll get you another plate,' she said, running out.

No expression of regret about the breakage, the curate thought to himself, it never even entered her head! Yet plates cost good money!

'You're surely not going to eat the cutlet?' his wife exclaimed as she came back in.

'What else would we do with it?'

'The cat could have it.'

'I'm not as well off as you appear to be,' he said, feeling miserable again. And there could have been another fine row if his wife had not kept quiet. But their happy mood was destroyed anyway.

The next day there was news of another amazing event: Rolandsen had disappeared. When he learned of the discovery in the forest and of Enoch's confession, he had burst out angrily: 'Hell! At least a month too soon!' Børre the organ-blower had heard him. Later that evening Rolandsen was nowhere to be found, neither in nor out. But Børre's boat, that had been moored at the Vicarage quay, had vanished, complete with oars and fishing gear.

At Rosengaard Mack had been informed immediately of the burglar's true identity, but strangely enough he seemed in no hurry to come over and take up the affair. Old Mack probably knew what he was doing. Rolandsen had cheated him out of a reward that he would now have to pay out again, and the moment was not the most opportune. It was not in his character to appear niggardly when such a matter of honour was involved, but the fact was that he was temporarily in slight financial embarrassment. His many business concerns required considerable outlay, and cash was no longer flowing in. His huge consignments of herring were still with an agent in Bergen, but prices were too low and he was not selling. Mack was waiting impatiently for the Indian summer, after which all the fishing came to an end and prices usually rose sky high. And the Russians were at war, so agriculture in that huge country would be neglected and the populace would be in need of herring.

For several weeks he avoided coming to the factory. Had he not also promised the curate's wife a bakery, and what could he say to her at present? The foundations were laid and the ground levelled, but nothing was being constructed. People began to gossip about him again, saying that the bakery scheme was probably causing him difficulties. The baker over at the mayor's place had even taken up drinking again. He felt safe; it would require more than a few days to build a bakery, he had time for a bit of a binge. The curate got to hear of the man's relapse and made a personal appeal to him; but it did no good, so secure did he feel.

And the truth was that the hard-working curate had quite enough to do. Though he never spared himself, he always had a backlog of work. Now one of his helpers had gone, Enoch, the most zealous of all. Levion had come to him only a couple of days after Enoch's fall from grace and had been very anxious to be reinstated.

'You can see that there's no one more suited to be a helper than I am,' he said to the curate.

'You're under suspicion of having started the fire.'

'Only a thief and a scoundrel would have told such a lie!' Levion exclaimed.

'Very well, then. But even so, I shan't be wanting you as a helper again.'

'Who will it be this time, then?'

'Nobody. I shall do without.'

That was the kind of man the curate was, strong and unyielding and fair to all. He had reason now to punish himself without mercy. The constant domestic unpleasantness and the many difficulties of his office were demoralising him and tempting him to abandon his calling. From time to time he had unpardonable thoughts. What would it matter, for instance, if he made his peace with Levion, who could do him some favours in return? Or, Mack at Rosengaard had offered his help for the worthy and needy — well, he, the curate, was the most poverty-stricken in the village; he could turn to Mack on behalf of a family in need and then just keep the aid given. And there were the shoes for his wife. He needed a few things himself too, some books, a philosophy; he was withering up in his daily toil and not developing spiritually. Rolandsen, that loud-mouthed rascal, had put the idea into his wife's head that it was human beings who had made God what He was. He wanted to prepare himself to refute Rolandsen and silence him when the next opportunity arose.

Mack appeared at long last — as usual in grand and stately fashion, with his daughter Elise by his side. He called at the Vicarage first of all, not only a courtesy-call, but also to show that he was not trying to wriggle out of his promise. The curate's wife asked about the bakery. Mack expressed regret that the work had not gone faster, but there were good reasons: the bakery could quite simply not be built this year, because the foundations had to have time to settle. She gave a little cry of disappointment, but the curate was rather relieved.

'That's what the experts tell me,' said Mack, 'and I have to follow their advice. The foundation walls might move several inches in the thaw next spring, and then what would happen to the building above?'

'Yes, what would happen?' the curate agreed.

Mack was no longer dejected. On the contrary, the Indian summer had drawn to a close, the herring fishing had come to a complete end, and a telegram from the agent had advised him that prices were shooting up. Mack could not resist telling them that at the Vicarage. In return, the curate was able to tell him where Rolandsen was hiding: on an island in the outer skerries, far out to the west on the open seaboard, living like a savage. A man and a woman had come to the Vicarage and brought the news to the curate.

Mack sent a boat out for Rolandsen immediately.

# 13

The fact was that Enoch's confession had caught Rolandsen unprepared. He was free now, but he did not have the four hundred crowns to repay Mack. That was why he took Børre's boat with all its fishing lines and tackle and rowed out into the dark and silent night. He headed for the outer skerries, a good ten miles, partly across open sea. He rowed the whole night long and sought out a suitable island at daybreak. He put ashore, setting a myriad of birds into flight around him.

He was hungry, and his first thought was to collect a dozen or two gulls' eggs to make a meal. But embryo chicks were forming in all of them. So he rowed out to do some fishing and was more successful. He lived on fish from day to day and sang and whiled the time away and ruled over the island. When it rained he took shelter beneath a splendid overhanging rock. At night he slept on a patch of grass and the sun never set.

Two weeks passed, then three. Rolandsen grew desperately thin from this wretched way of life, but his eyes burned fiercer and fiercer from sheer determination, and he had no intention of giving in. His one fear was that someone would come and disturb him. A few nights ago a boat had drawn near, rowed by a man and a woman who were obviously collecting down. They would have landed on the island, but Rolandsen prevented them; he had seen them coming from afar and had time to work up a rage, so that when they arrived he was whirling Børre's little anchor about so threateningly that they rowed away again in fright. Rolandsen grinned to himself, and his emaciated features took on the appearance of a sinister devil.

One morning the birds were making more noise than usual and woke Rolandsen up; it was so early that it was still really night. He could see a boat approaching, already quite close. The trouble with Rolandsen was that he was so slow to anger. Here was this boat coming, at a highly inconvenient moment for him, but by the time he had worked up a proper fury it had already landed — otherwise he might have been able to stop the intruders with a fusillade of stones.

Two of Mack's men from the factory, father and son, stepped ashore. 'Good morning,' said the older one.

'I can't say I'm pleased to see you and I warn you I may have to do something about it,' Rolandsen replied.

'And what might that be?' said the man, looking across only half-confidently at his son.

'I could strangle you to death, if you like. How would that appeal to you?'

'We've been sent by Mack himself to find you.'

'Of course you've come from Mack. I know what he wants.'

The younger man joined in at that point and said that Børre wanted his boat and his fishing gear back.

Rolandsen exclaimed bitterly: 'Him? Is the man mad? What about me? I'm living on a barren island, I have to have a boat to get to people, and I have to have fishing lines to live. Tell him that from me.'

'And then we've got a message from the new man at the telegraph station that there are some important telegrams waiting for you.'

Rolandsen gave a start. What? Already! He asked another couple of questions, got their answers, and made no more objections to returning with them. The young man rowed Børre's boat and Rolandsen sat in the older man's.

In the bow there was a box which aroused a ravenous hope in Rolandsen that it might contain food. He wanted to ask whether they had any food with them, but he restrained himself out of sheer pride, and tried to distract himself by talking.

'How did Mack find out I was here?'

'Someone reported seeing you. A man and a woman had come here one night. They'd been quite frightened.'

106

'Well, what were they doing here anyway? I've found a good new fishing ground by that island. And now I'm having to abandon it.'

'How long had you thought of staying there?'

'None of your business,' said Rolandsen curtly. He looked at the food-box, and could contain himself no longer: 'That's an extraordinarily ugly box, not one you'd want to keep any food in, I shouldn't think. What's it for?'

'If I only had all the meat and cheese and butter there'd been in that box, I wouldn't be short of food for many years to come,' the man replied.

Rolandsen hawked loudly and spat in the sea.

'When did the telegrams arrive?' he asked.

'Oh, quite a while ago now.'

Halfway back they drew the two boats alongside one another and father and son began eating from the box. Rolandsen gazed in every direction but theirs. The older man said: 'We've got some food here, if it's good enough for you.' And they handed Rolandsen the whole box.

He waved it away and said: 'I ate half an hour ago and I'm full up. You don't know how well baked that bread looks, though. No thanks, I just wanted to see it, have a sniff of it.' He went on prattling away, addressing himself to the four winds: 'We live pretty well up here in the north. I'm sure there's not a single shed that doesn't have a haunch of meat hanging in it, and there's as much ham around as anyone could need. But it makes you feel like an animal to want to eat so much!'

He turned reluctantly to face them: 'How long would I have stayed there, did you ask? I would have stayed till the autumn, of course, and seen the shooting stars. I love strange events, it amuses me to see a planet break into pieces.'

'I don't really understand what you mean.'

'A planet. When one star smashes into another and lights up the entire sky.'

But the men carried on eating, until suddenly Rolandsen could hold back no more: 'What pigs you are! Look how much you're stuffing yourselves with!'

'We've finished now,' the older man said placatingly.

The boats separated and the two men took up the oars again. Rolandsen lay down to sleep.

They arrived back in the afternoon and he went straight up to the telegraph station for his telegrams. They bore encouraging news about his invention, a substantial offer for the patent from Hamburg, and an even higher bid from another firm through the Patent Office. And Rolandsen was such a weird fellow that he ran off into the forest and stayed there alone for some long time before he turned his thoughts to finding some food. His emotion had made him a boy again, a child sitting quietly with folded arms.

# 14

Rolandsen made his way to Mack's office, advancing like a man raised from the dead, like a lion. It would be an odd sensation for Mack and his family to see him again. Perhaps Elise would congratulate him, and such sincere friendship would do him a power of good.

But he was disappointed. He met Elise outside the factory talking to her brother, and she took so little notice of him that she hardly even responded to his greeting. The two just continued their conversation. Rolandsen did not disturb them and did not ask after Mack. He went up to the office and knocked on the door. It was locked. He came back down again and said: 'Your father sent for me; do you know where I can find him?'

They were in no hurry to answer, finishing what

they had to say first. Then Fredrik replied: 'My father's up at the sluice-gates.'

They could have told me that when I arrived, Rolandsen thought to himself. They were both completely indifferent to him, they had let him go on up to the office without saying a word.

'Could you send a message to him?' Rolandsen asked.

Fredrik spoke slowly: 'When my father's up at the sluice it's because he has things to do there.'

Rolandsen looked at them both in surprise.

'You'll have to come back later,' said Fredrik.

Rolandsen acquiesced and started to leave.

But then he began to bite his lips and think about it. Suddenly he turned round and said without further ado: 'I have to say that the only reason I've come here is to meet your father.'

'Well, come back later,' said Fredrik.

'If I come back a second time it'll be to say I won't be coming a third.'

Fredrik shrugged his shoulders.

'Here's father now,' said Elise.

Old Mack was walking towards them. He furrowed his brow, spoke brusquely and went ahead of Rolandsen to the office. He was far from courteous. 'I offered you a chair last time. This time I won't.'

'No, no,' said Rolandsen. But he still did not understand the reason for Mack's anger.

Mack found it unpleasant to be harsh. He had power over this man who had wronged him, but he wanted to show himself superior by not using it. 'You know what has happened, of course?'

Rolandsen replied: 'I've been away. Things may have happened here that you know about but I don't.'

'Then I'll bring you up to date,' said Mack. And now he was like a little god, with a man's fate in his hands. 'Did you say that you burned my insurance policy?'

'Well, actually,' Rolandsen began, 'if you're going to start asking me lots of questions . . .'

'Here it is,' said Mack, bringing out the document. 'The money has been found too. The whole lot was wrapped in a scarf that did not belong to you.'

Rolandsen made no protest.

Mack went on: 'It belonged to Enoch.'

Rolandsen had to smile at all this solemnity and said jestingly: 'You'll probably find it was Enoch who was the thief, then.'

Mack was not amused by the joke, it was not even expressed with due respect. 'You've made a fool of me,' he said, 'and cheated me out of four hundred crowns.'

Rolandsen, with his invaluable telegrams in his pocket, still found it hard to be serious. 'Let's talk about it a little more,' he said.

Mack's response was sharp: 'I forgave you last time. I shall not do so now.'

'I can pay you the money back.'

Mack was outraged. 'It's still not the money that matters to me. You're a swindler, don't you realise that?'

'Will you allow me to explain?'

111

'No.'

'That's completely unreasonable,' said Rolandsen, still smiling. 'What do you want of me then?'

'I'm going to have you arrested,' answered Mack.

Fredrik came in at that point and took up his place at the desk. He had heard the last words and saw his father in a rare state of agitation.

Rolandsen put his hand into his pocket where he had the telegrams and said: 'Won't you accept the money?'

'No,' said Mack. 'You can hand it over to the authorities.'

Rolandsen just stood there, a lion no longer. When all was said and done he had committed an offence, and he could be imprisoned for it. All right. When Mack looked at him enquiringly, as if wondering why he was still standing there, he responded: 'I'm waiting to be arrested.'

Mack was taken aback. 'Here and now? No, you can go home and get ready.'

'Thank you. I have a few telegrams to send.'

Mack was mollified by these words: he was not a monster, after all. 'You can have today and tomorrow to get yourself ready,' he said.

Rolandsen bowed and left.

Elise was still standing outside and he went past her without acknowledgement. What was lost was lost, there was nothing to be done about it.

But Elise called softly after him—he stopped in amazement and confusion and stood gaping at her.

'I only wanted to say . . . I don't suppose it's particularly serious.'

It was all beyond him, he did not even understand why she was talking to him at all. 'I'm being allowed to go home,' he said. 'I'm going to send off a few telegrams.'

She drew closer to him, her breast heaving, looking around her uneasily. 'I suppose my father was very angry. But I'm sure it will soon blow over.'

Rolandsen felt annoyed. Did he have no rights himself? 'Your father can do as he pleases,' he retorted.

Well! But still breathing heavily, she said: 'Why are you looking at me like that? Don't you recognise me?'

He was certainly in favour today! 'Recognise or not recognise, it all seems to depend on people's mood.'

A pause. Then at last Elise said: 'But you have to admit that what you did . . . Still, it's worse for you.'

'All right, so it's worse for me. I'm not going to let myself be attacked by all and sundry. Your father can have me arrested if he likes.'

Without a word she turned and went.

He waited two days, he waited three, but nobody came to the organ-blower's house to fetch him. He was in a state of great tension. He had written his telegrams and was ready to send them the moment he was arrested. He would accept the highest offer for his invention and sell the patent. In the meantime he was not idle, he was keeping the foreign firms busy with negotiations about various things, including the purchase of the waterfall above Mack's factory and guarantees of transport rights. All these matters were for the time being entirely in his hands.

But Mack was not the sort to persecute a fellow-creature. On the contrary, his business was going well again and in prosperous times it pleased him much more to be excessively benevolent. Another telegram from the agent in Bergen had informed him that the herring had been sold to Russia. If Mack wanted money, it was at his disposal. He felt on top of things again.

When more than a week had passed and nothing had happened, Rolandsen returned to Mack's office. He was worn out with the anxiety and uncertainty, and he wanted a decision.

'I've been ready for a week now and you haven't had me arrested,' he said.

'Well, young man, I've been reconsidering,' Mack replied patronisingly.

'Well, old man, you'd better decide now,' said Rolandsen angrily. 'You may think you can go on waiting for ever and lavish your favours as you please, but I shall do something about it. I'll turn myself in.'

'I would have expected a rather different attitude from you today.'

'I'll show you what attitude you can expect,' Rolandsen shouted with unnecessary arrogance, and threw his telegrams down in front of Mack. His nose looked even bigger now that his face was so much thinner.

Mack cast his eyes over the telegrams. 'So you're an

inventor!' But as he looked further his eyes narrowed and he read more carefully. 'Fish-glue?' he said at last. Then he began studying the telegrams again. 'This all seems very promising,' he went on, glancing up at Rolandsen. 'Are you really being offered such a large sum for an invention of a fish-glue process?'

'Yes.'

'Well, I congratulate you. But now you should be magnanimous enough not to be discourteous to an old man.'

'Yes, you're right, of course. But I've been pretty shattered by all this worry. You said you were going to have me arrested, but nothing's come of it.'

'No—I'll have to tell you what happened. Someone intervened. I was going to do it.'

'Who intervened?'

'Well, you know what women are like. I have a daughter. Elise said no.'

'How strange,' said Rolandsen.

Mack looked at the telegrams again. 'This is splendid. Can you tell me something about your invention?'

Rolandsen described it in outline.

'So in a way we're competitors now,' said Mack.

'Not just in a way. From the moment I send off my replies we'll be competitors in earnest.'

'What?' exclaimed Mack, disconcerted. 'What do you mean by that? Are you going to start manufacturing?'

'Yes. There's a waterfall above yours, a much bigger one. It wouldn't even need a sluice-gate.'

115

'That's Levion's waterfall.'

'I've bought it.'

Mack wrinkled his brow in thought. 'All right,' he said, 'let's be competitors.'

'You'll be the loser,' said Rolandsen.

This kind of talk was beginning to irritate the great Mack more and more. He was not accustomed to it and would not tolerate it. 'I'm surprised you keep forgetting that you're still in my hands,' he said.

'Report me then. My turn will come later.'

'What will you do?'

'I'll ruin you.'

Fredrik came in to the office. He could see straight away that there had been an argument, and he was angry that his father didn't just sort out the dismissed telegraph-operator with the prominent nose once and for all.

Rolandsen raised his voice and said: 'I'll make you an offer. We can exploit this invention together. We can convert your factory and I can take over as manager. My offer holds good for twenty-four hours!'

With that, Rolandsen left the telegrams on the desk and stalked out.

# 15

Autumn had arrived, the wind was blowing through the forest, the sea was turning brown and cold, and the stars were sparkling more brightly in the sky. But Ove Rolandsen had no time to gaze at shooting stars any more, though he continued to be fascinated by such phenomena. There had been lots of building labourers at Mack's factory lately, demolishing in one place and constructing in another, according to specifications laid down by Rolandsen, who was in charge of the enterprise. He had overcome all difficulties and had now achieved great respect.

'I basically believed in that chap all along,' said Old Mack.

'I didn't,' said proud Elise. 'But what a man he's become. It feels as though he has saved us.'

'Well, I wouldn't say it's as bad as that,' Mack

answered.

'He says hello, but he doesn't wait for a response. He just goes on by.'

'He's very busy.'

'He's wormed his way into the family, that's what he's done,' said Elise, her lips tight. 'Wherever we go, he's there too. But if he has any ideas about me, he's making a big mistake.'

And Elise travelled back to town.

Everything went on as usual; it seemed as if she was not missed. But as far as Rolandsen was concerned, he had promised himself that from the moment he went into partnership with Mack he would work solidly and not spend time dreaming of other things. Summer is the time for dreaming, and then you have to stop. But some people go on dreaming all their lives, and cannot change. There was Miss van Loos in Bergen, for instance. Rolandsen had had a letter from her to say she no longer regarded him as beneath her, since he had not besmirched his character with an act of burglary after all, but had just been playing tricks. And she took back her decision to break off the relationship, if it wasn't too late.

Elise Mack came home in October. It was rumoured that she was definitely engaged now, and that her fiancé, Henrik Burnus Henriksen, captain of the coastal steamer, was paying her visits. There was to be a ball at Rosengaard, and a German band on their way home from a tour in the far north had been hired to play their flutes and horns in the great hall. The whole village was invited, Rolandsen among them, and Olga the sexton's daughter was going too, and would be received as Fredrik's future wife. But the curate and his wife would not be able to attend. A new vicar had been appointed, was indeed expected any day, and the good curate was moving north, where another parish awaited his care. He was not averse to going to plough and sow in new soil; it had not been an unmitigated pleasure working here. He could look back on one major achievement: he had got Levion's sister to remember the particular man who had a duty to marry her. It was the village carpenter, a house-owner with a bit of money under his pillow. When the curate joined them in matrimony before the altar, it gave him a certain satisfaction. There were after all some occasions when unremitting toil bore fruit.

Life had to be taken one day at a time. The Lord be praised! the curate thought. His household was in somewhat better order again. The new housekeeper had arrived, and she was elderly and reliable. He wanted to take her with him and retain her services when they moved. Everything would work out. The curate had been an obstinate man, but there seemed to be no feelings of resentment against him. When he boarded the boat down at the Vicarage landing-stage, quite a crowd had gathered to see him off. As for Rolandsen, he did not want to miss the opportunity of displaying his good manners: although Mack's boat was waiting for him with three men on board, he delayed joining them until the curate and his wife had finally gone. Despite everything, the curate felt obliged to thank him for this courtesy. And as Levion had lifted the curate's wife ashore when they landed, he was granted the same honour now. There was every sign of improved fortunes for him too — the curate had promised to do what he could to get him reinstated as lay-helper.

All things would come right in the end.

'If you weren't going north and I weren't going south, we could have kept company on the voyage,' said Rolandsen.

'Yes,' replied the curate. 'But let us remember, my dear Rolandsen, that whether we go to the north or go to the south, we shall all meet again in the same place in the end!' Thus did he bear witness, unremitting to the last.

His wife sat in the stern, wearing the same pathetic shoes. They had been patched, but that only made them look more disreputable. But she was not depressed by it; her eyes were shining and she was pleased to be going to a new place and to see new things. Though her thoughts turned sadly to a large pebble that the curate had prevented her packing in her trunk even though it was so pretty.

So they departed, and there was much waving of hats and sou'westers and handkerchiefs and cries of farewell from boat and shore.

Then Rolandsen went on board. He had to be at Rosengaard that evening; there was a double engagement to be celebrated and he did not want to miss this further opportunity to display his good manners. Since Mack's boat had no pennant on the mast, he had borrowed a magnificent red and white one from another boat, and he got the men to hoist it before they set off.

He arrived in good time. It was obvious that there were festivities going on at this great trading-station: the windows were lit on both floors and the ships in the harbour were flying their flags although it was already quite dark. He told his men to go ashore and send three other men to replace them; he would be wanting to return to the factory at midnight.

Rolandsen was immediately received by Fredrik, who was in fine spirits: he now had every hope of getting the job as mate on the coastal steamer; then he would be able to marry and make something of himself. Old Mack was happy too, and was wearing the decoration the king had given him when he had made a royal visit to this northern province of Finnmark. Neither Elise nor Captain Henriksen was anywhere to be seen; they were no doubt billing and cooing in a room by themselves.

Rolandsen drank a couple of glasses to put himself in a strong and silent mood. He sat down with Old Mack and talked about various business concerns. There was the dye he had discovered, which had seemed insignificant but was now probably going to become their principal product. He needed machinery and distillation apparatus.

Then Elise came walking by, looked Rolandsen full

in the face, nodded and said 'Good evening.' He stood up and returned her greeting, but she went on past.

'She's very busy this evening,' said Mack.

'So we have to have everything completely ready before the Lofoten fishing season begins,' said Rolandsen, resuming his seat. He was not to be unsettled by even the slightest disquietude. 'I still think we should charter a small steamer and have Fredrik as the skipper.'

'Fredrik may be getting another post now. But we can talk more about that later; we've got till tomorrow.'

'I'm going back at midnight.'

'Surely not!' exclaimed Mack.

Rolandsen stood up and repeated curtly: 'At midnight!' That's how decisive and unyielding he was going to be.

'I thought you would be certain to stay the night. On an occasion like this. I venture to call it a special occasion.'

They walked round among the rest of the company, stopping to chat from time to time. When Rolandsen met Captain Henriksen they drank together as if they were old friends, even though they had never met before. The captain was a good-natured, rather stout man.

Then the music began, and they took their places at the tables laid out in three rooms. Rolandsen was sensible enough to choose a place away from the grandest guests. Old Mack found him there as he made his round of the tables. 'So that's where you're sitting.

Well, I'd rather thought . . .'

Rolandsen replied: 'Thanks very much, but we'll be able to hear your speech all right from here.'

Mack shook his head. 'No, I'm not going to make a speech.' He went off with a pensive look on his face, as if there might be some kind of problem.

The meal progressed, with much wine and a great buzz of conversation. When coffee came Rolandsen started drafting a telegram. It was to Miss van Loos in Bergen, to say that it was not too late: Come north as soon as you can. Yours, Ove.

It was all right, everything was all right, wonderful! He took the telegram to the telegraph station himself and made sure it was despatched. Then he returned. People were livelier at the tables now, moving about and changing places. Elise came over to him and proffered her hand. She apologised for not having stopped to talk earlier.

'I just have to say how beautiful you look this evening,' he said, confidently and courteously.

'Do you think so?'

'I've always thought so. I'm an old admirer of yours, as I'm sure you've realised. Don't you remember last year when I actually proposed to you?'

She did not seem to like this turn of the conversation, and walked off. But he came across her again a little later on. Fredrik had led off the dancing with his fiancée, the ball had begun, so no one took any notice of the two of them talking together.

Elise said: 'By the way, I can convey greetings from

an old acquaintance of yours, Miss van Loos.'

'Really?'

'She'd heard that I'm getting married and asked if she could be my housekeeper. She's said to be very competent. But then you know her much better than I do.'

'She certainly is very good at her job, yes. But I'm afraid she can't be your housekeeper.'

'Why ever not?'

'Because I sent her a telegram this evening and offered her a different post. She's engaged to me now.'

Proud Elise was taken aback, and stared at him. 'I thought it was all over between the two of you,' she said.

'Well, you know what they say about old love . . . It was over once, but . . .'

'I see,' she said.

'I must tell you that you've never looked so lovely as this evening!' he said, with grandiloquent politeness. 'And your dress, that dark red velvet!' He felt satisfied with these words too. No one could suspect the least uneasiness behind them.

'You didn't seem to like her all that much,' she said.

He noticed that her eyes were moist, and was some-what disconcerted. Her slightly husky voice also confused him, and his expression altered.

'What's become of your serene composure now?' she exclaimed, and smiled.

'You've taken it away,' he mumbled.

Suddenly she stroked his hand, just the once, and

left him. She hurried through the rooms, seeing nobody and hearing nothing, rushing straight ahead. Her brother was standing in the passageway and called to her; she turned her smiling face towards him and tears started flowing from her eyes. Then she ran off up the stairs to her room.

A quarter of an hour later her father came in to her. She flung her arms round his neck and said: 'No, I can't go through with it.'

'There, there. No, no. But you must come down again and dance. People are asking after you. And what have you said to Rolandsen? He's completely changed. Have you been rude to him again?'

'No, I haven't been rude to him.'

'Because if you have, you must put things right immediately. He's leaving at midnight.'

'Midnight?' Elise was ready in a second, and said: 'I'm coming now.'

She went downstairs and found Captain Henriksen. 'I can't,' she said.

He made no reply.

'So much the worse for me, perhaps, but I'm sorry, I simply can't.'

'All right,' was all he said.

She could think of no further explanation to give, and since the captain's response was so laconic, no more was said. Elise went to the telegraph station and sent a telegram to Miss van Loos in Bergen telling her not to accept Ove Rolandsen's offer because once again it was not seriously meant. Await letter. Elise Mack.

Then she went home and joined in the dancing again. 'Is it true that you're going back at midnight?' she asked Rolandsen.

'Yes.'

'I'll come with you to the factory. There's something I've got to do there.'

And she stroked his hand again.